THE ARTIST OF THE MISSING

FARRAR, STRAUS AND GIROUX   NEW YORK

THE ARTIST OF THE MISSING

PAUL LAFARGE

ILLUSTRATIONS BY STEPHEN ALCORN

Farrar, Straus and Giroux
19 Union Square West, New York 10003

Distributed in Canada by Douglas & McIntyre Ltd.
Printed in the United States of America
Designed by Fritz Metsch
First edition, 1999
Illustrations © by Stephen Alcorn

Library of Congress Cataloging-in-Publication Data
LaFarge, Paul.
    The artist of the missing / Paul LaFarge
        p.   cm.
    ISBN 0-374-52580-3
    I. Title
    PS3562.A269A89   1999
    813'.54—dc21   98-32152

to my forebears, for bears, and bearing with

*None of the things therefore which seem
to be lost is utterly lost, since nature replenishes
one thing out of another and does not suffer
anything to be begotten, before she has been
recruited by the death of another.*

—LUCRETIUS

THE ARTIST OF THE MISSING

IMAGINE THAT A DEAD MAN ARRIVES IN A city. For days he stumbles about, the way the dead, if they came back to life, might stumble from their graves: pale and puffy-eyed as though they'd slept badly, rubbing a three days' growth of stubble and wondering what place this was, and whether it was the one they had never expected to reach. Whether or not it is that place, the city is large and full of marvels. The dead man wanders from one to the next, astounded by everything: here is the garden where the trees take on the form of fleeing lovers, and here the palace in the shape of a clock, where the spires sound the hour at noon and at midnight. In this neighborhood all paths lead toward the river, and in this other they lead nowhere, but ramify into courts and cul-de-sacs scrounged by cats, places where the sun sets its foot only twice a year. What a wonder this city is, the dead man thinks, and what a shame that we have nothing like it among the dead! For these people are always finding something new, whereas the dead have ceased to invent, and make do with the first forms that came to their hands long ago, when even death was novel and anything might have happened. The dead man can hardly sleep: he must see the entire city from spire to sewer and harbor to hill. Any day now, a messenger will come to take him back to the land of the dead. I'd better hurry, he thinks, so that if I must go back, at least I'll have stories to tell. At the end of a week he has seen enough to last a lifetime, but the messenger does not come. The dead man has never been so happy: he goes out at sunrise and comes home long after dusk. In a month, he has seen something of the city, but not the greatest part, nor even, he thinks, the most beautiful. So many streets remain to be discovered, so many buildings which appear at the edge of his view, then vanish again when he turns a corner. When the messenger comes for him at last, he says, I'm not ready. Give me another month and I'll have seen enough.

At the end of the second month the dead man sighs: the city is larger than he thought at first, much larger! Why, just the other day a café waiter was telling him that there is a museum devoted entirely to thread, and another to candles; they face each other across a green canal, the least tributary of a system of canals which goes everywhere, and for almost nothing you can visit it by boat! The dead man can't leave until he's seen the canal and the twin museums. And then there's the library, which he visited only long enough to read an out-of-date magazine, and the race-track with its Sunday smell of sod, where he has not placed even the smallest bet! How will he explain that to the dead? No, no, I can't go back yet, he tells the messenger, give me two months more. When the messenger comes two months later, the dead man only shakes his head, No, don't bother me, I must hurry if I want to see even a bit of the city! Today I'm going to the harbor, and tomorrow, if the weather holds, I'll see the tanneries—I mean the old tanneries; I don't know when I'll find time to see the new ones. Six more months will barely be enough; I'll have to rush and won't see anything as well as I would have liked.

Six months later the dead man is bone-tired, but when the messenger comes for him he snaps, Not yet, not yet! The city's playing tricks on me. When I set out toward something new it shows me only old things, streets I've already seen, and the rest hangs back, just out of sight, like a coy understudy! Give me a year, no, give me five, and I will see through its ruses somehow. The messenger comes back at the end of five years and finds the dead man in his room, slumped in an armchair with his back to the window. Is that all? the messenger asks. Have you seen the whole city? The dead man shakes his head. You might as well take me back now, he says, for I've been here six years and haven't seen anything at all.

The strange thing is that after they return to the land of the dead, arm in arm, the dead man's sleep is broken by wonderful dreams: he sees the city's spires turn red at dusk, and smells the perfume of the night-blooming plants; he walks by the river in the morning when fog hides the other bank, and at midday sits in a square where old men chase the sun away with fans. What was the city like? clamor the dead. Tell us! Tell us! To which the dead man replies only: You must see it for yourselves. And, one by one, they do.

PRUDENCE

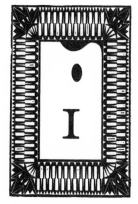

FRANK AND JAMES SHARED A ROOM AT Bellaway's, a boardinghouse for itinerant judges which accepted transients in the off-season. Their room, a garret, with walls covered in green paper that reeked of wool in the humid weather, was still inhabited by the last occupant's furniture. A botanist he had been, said Mrs. Bellaway, and unlucky in love. One night he tied his albums of pressed flowers to his chest and threw himself into the river, so that, she said, the flowers swelled with water and bloomed again; a trail of rehydrated petals followed his body all the way downstream to the harbor. Aside from the petals, the botanist had left behind a bed and sofa, a bookshelf, and a supply of the pins, weights, glues, and papers useful in the preservation of plants. —You can keep it all, if you like, Mrs. Bellaway told them; but extra blankets're a dollar each. While James negotiated with her, Frank picked the botanist's implements up, one after the other. They seemed to belong to another world, older and more complete than the one he had left: a world in which not even weeds were allowed to fade, wither, and disappear. A little frightened by the power such a world must possess, he let the brass mountings and gummed labels fall from his hands, and turned to the window, a dormer with a deep sill and small panes. When he sat on the sill and curled his neck under the eaves, the window formed a sort of room all its own. From this vantage he could see the beginning of the city: the dull brick backs and tar-paper roofs of the row houses opposite and the top branches of some gangly and leafless trees which suggested a garden and a courtyard below. Beyond the first rank of houses a second rose up, and beyond that a third, with crenellations of white stone. Above their tops he could make out spires and squat water tanks and the parallel lines of the towers of glass which, he had heard, rose above the winter fogs and summer storms to glitter in per-petual sunlight. Beyond the towers was only haze, the chestnut smoke of the factories on the riverbanks, factories he had hitherto known only as names stamped on objects, tools, pots and plates, all of which had been sold off what already seemed a long time ago. Turning from the window, Frank took a photograph from his bag. It showed a man and a woman walking arm in arm up a street which might have been the one next to Bellaway's. When he held the photograph to the window, however, he saw that the real street was brighter and far wider than the pictured one. He put the photo back in his bag and went to see how James was get-ting on with Mrs. Bellaway.

Between James's savings and the money Frank had made from the auction, there was no pressing need for them to work. They spent their days walking from monument to monument, stopping in the shade of a café when the midafternoon heat clotted the air. They followed a guidebook which had once belonged to Frank's father, but the book must have been old, or else the city had recently changed. The guidebook urged them: *Be sure to pay your respects to the bears who have their own island in the zoo. They will swim to you if you hold out a fish, and take it from your hand as gently as you please*—but of the bears they could find no trace. Instead, they spent an afternoon admiring the puffins, magnificent birds with white bellies and the faces of clowns. *After a day at the zoo you're sure to be tired*, the guidebook said, *so why not stop in Wardens' Square for some tea?* Wardens' Square turned out to be a dingy court covered with netting to keep out flies and sun; there was no tea to be found there, though the shop windows displayed a variety of elegant, slightly used machines. It was the same everywhere: in place of great wonders they found small marvels, and vice versa, so that they were never sure where they had gone or what they had seen, though it always seemed to them that they saw more than they'd expected. Long after it became clear that the guidebook was of no practical use, Frank insisted on bringing it with him. When they stopped before one monument, he read the description of another, demolished long ago, which had stood in the same spot, as though he could not stand to see the city only as it was, but must double its real sights with imaginary ones.

Frank decided to teach himself to draw. He bought a sketchbook from a stationer's near the bus terminal, a place that sold blank books of all descriptions. In the late afternoon, when the light turned copper-red and the shadows blue, he sat in the win-

dow of their room at Bellaway's and copied the city onto one page after another. He began with buildings, because they were large and did not move. Slowly, the apartment house opposite grew clotheslines and chimney pots; its red-brick rear appeared first as a texture of smudges; then cornices revealed their curves to Frank's hand, and the windows arranged themselves in floors and columns. Evening rose, erasing detail, until all that remained were the lit rectangles, near and distant, where other lives took place. A man opened letters; a woman stirred a pot; an old gentleman talked on the telephone. Blinds rose and fell; shadows crossed the rooms, embraced, parted; lights went off and came on again. In a yellow room opposite and a little below his own, a naked woman combed her hair. She turned, and Frank saw the minuscule profile of her breast, the sweep of her hip half hidden by her long black hair. She left the window's yellow frame and came back, turned toward him and raised her arms to secure her hair with an invisible pin. The room went dark soon after. Frank tried to draw her, but his hand could not make her out; his sketches were a jumble of black hair, yellow walls, a pale arm, a vase on a table. He threw them away, but continued to watch her window. Her hours were irregular. Some nights she came home early, others at dawn; sometimes her window was dark for nights on end.

Her half-seen figure chased the familiar faces from Frank's dreams. He woke feeling light-headed, as though a space were being cleared in the clutter of his old affections. Traffic groaned around a distant roundabout; the air reeked of pollen and Bellaway's bitter coffee; the country seemed as far-off as the city in the guidebook. In his sketches, the spires caught the sun; the clocks struck the hour; line by line the city came to life. The woman in the window was still too far away to draw, but Frank had other occasions to study the human figure. While he sat upstairs sketching buildings, James had been downstairs in Bellaway's parlor, teaching the transients one lurching rustic dance after another. James unpacked his guitar and sang for them the long songs, almost like stories, with which country dwellers entertained themselves at night. He was good-looking in a babyish sort of way; there was a roundness to his chin and lips which suggested that his face had not lost all that men's faces lose between boyhood and the age of twenty-five or thirty. He danced confidently, and had a clear voice. The transients applauded and called for more; even the Great Evan, a magician who made a seasonal living pulling scarves from tourists' sleeves, was enchanted. James introduced Frank to Charles, Bellaway's hunchbacked caretaker, who had been a signals clerk in the Navy and had three daughters by a foreign wife, Glenda, now deceased. The daughters came to Bellaway's each week to help their father with the housekeeping. They were taken with the handsome stranger who could begin one song without, it seemed, ending the last, so that his voice played on for hours, turning the parlor into a windy plain, the couches into horses, and the mantel into mountains. The daughters' names were Rosalyn, Evelyn, and Carolyn, a consonance which none of them appreciated as much as had their late mother, who had been some sort of poet overseas. When they had done folding and dusting, scrubbing the tureens and plucking weeds from the garden, they rested in the parlor, the three of them in a row on the longest of Mrs. Bellaway's sofas.

Carolyn was the most beautiful: her doll's face and heating-coil

THE ARTIST OF THE MISSING

curls looked as though they were molded fresh every morning. Her slender figure promised immunity to the wear of time and chores. Not so Evelyn, the youngest, who perused the world as though it were a book, and one printed small besides, so that she had to stoop and squint to make any sense of it. When she relaxed, as she did when James sang, her eyes opened wide and her face took on an air of perfect incomprehension. Rosalyn, the middle daughter, was beautiful only in her hands, which were long, slender, and rose-white. She knew it, too, and made every effort to keep them from being worn down, avoiding heavy chores, though she wasn't averse to kneeling in the garden and snipping with long shears at the rosebushes. Rosalyn never squinted at the world as Evelyn did, nor did she watch it, like Carolyn, with wide-open doll's eyes. Drifting half in and half out of attentiveness, she was the one whom James's singing moved the most; his wonderful stories became more wonderful still in her spotty attention, as she filled in the parts she'd missed with dreams of her own.

When James told them that Frank was an artist, they insisted on having their portraits done. First Carolyn and then the other two posed for him. Frank's first sketches were nearly his last; his clumsy hands brought out the slight but unmistakable resemblance which the daughters bore to their hunchbacked father. As he learned proportion, though, their figures grew girlish again, until at last their father had been almost entirely erased, and Glenda—who had been a rare beauty—appeared the sole parent of all three. Impromptu sketches followed; Frank learned composition from the way they arranged themselves on the sofa, so that Carolyn, no matter where she sat, was always the most prominent, and Evelyn always the least in view. He owed his knowledge of gesture to Rosalyn's hands, and drew them again and again, to the delight of their owner, who seemed in those pictures to have stepped from her usual fog into a patch of hazy light, as though the beauty of her hands had made the rest of her beautiful as well. —Make me a copy of that one, said James, and so Frank learned to trace.

Charles had no use for artists any more than he did for plumbers; both of them, he said, would take your money in return for something you could teach yourself if only you had half a mind to learn it. It was the effacement of his own features from the portraits that won Charles over. The more Glenda appeared on the page, the more he respected the pictures and their maker. In the end he begrudged Frank something like awe, and deferred to his opinion not only on art but on questions of etiquette, sport, and weather, which embarrassed Frank continually.

When summer had fallen from the air like a sooty precipitate, Charles invited Frank and James to dinner at his house, in a part of the city where saplings lined the sidewalks and margins of brown grass separated one house from the next. Dinner scenes filled Frank's sketchbook the next morning. Charles held forth on the duties of a signals clerk, and James spread his arms as he told them how it was in the country; Rosalyn blushed furiously at her hands and James sat so close to her that their shoulders brushed each other; Evelyn squinted in one direction and Carolyn smiled in the other; Charles asked Frank whether he'd liked the dinner and how long he thought the good weather would last; he told them how he'd met Glenda on the far side of the ocean, and lost her not fifty feet from the door of his house, crushed by a bus which coasted past one foggy night. Glenda oh Glenda, he wept, as with one hand he motioned for Rosalyn to sit a little farther away from James. And Evelyn, through all of it, almost smiling, as though she'd seen this dinner many times before, and could tell you the menu of emotions it would consume: laughter with the soup, and tears with the tea. Riding home in Charles's car, Frank berated himself for having said nothing to impress the daughters, but he was a pitiably slow storyteller and had no talent for flattery. As he had said nothing, nothing could be decided about him, and this was his consolation.

Frank drew faces quickly now, and found details in his drawings that he had overlooked in their originals. He bought a box of charcoals, and in broad strokes rendered the part of the city where the buildings were made of iron, and the cellars filled each night with smoke and music. He taught himself to draw motion; James and Rosalyn danced across the page, their scattered limbs a flurry of pen strokes. He learned the rules of light and shade, and searchlights crosshatched the evening sky.

During the short season between summer and fall, when the leaves on the riverside trees glowed with golden veins, James and Rosalyn went walking through the secluded paths of the city's parks. Their walks grew into the shrinking evenings, and each night James returned less able to say where he'd been. One night he returned unable to tell Frank anything of what he had done; then he admitted that he and Rosalyn had fallen in love.

—We went to the aquarium, or was it the arboretum? And I told her, I can't think of anyone but you. She nodded, so I asked her, Can you think of anyone but me? She shook her head. So that's it. We're in love.

—That's wonderful, Frank said, and rose to congratulate his friend.

—There's only one problem. Charles doesn't think I have enough money to marry his daughter, so I need to ask a favor, Frank, if I can borrow your money? Just to show it to him, a little trick, you see? And then we'll all go out.

—Of course, Frank said, of course. It would, he reasoned, leave him two daughters all to himself, and though Carolyn had lost interest in him Frank thought that Evelyn might, once or twice, have smiled in a way that meant he, too, might soon depart on sightless walks.

James began to say something else, then saw that his friend's attention had been captured by the botanist's glue pots. He closed his mouth, smiled agreeably, and slept, as he always did, like a child.

It was James who suggested that they come to the city. James was the one who stood to inherit a farm and a lifetime of inexorable attachments; it was natural that he want to run away, only, as he pointed out, —Now that we're grown up they can't call it running away anymore. It's just moving on, and everyone does it, so why not us, now, Frank?

Because they were not running away they left in the late morning, having assured James's mother that they would be back by dusk. James meant to write a card when he arrived in the city, to let the family know that he was well, that Frank was well, that all was well, but first he had trouble buying stamps, then he couldn't think of what to say, then he didn't know how to say it; at last he forgot about it altogether. Frank did not remind him.

When Frank was five years old, his mother took him to stay with James. —It's only for a few days, she said; then she left, and never returned. When Frank asked where she had gone, James's father explained: Your parents have gone south, but we're happy to have you, and besides, where else would you go? He told Frank stories of the south, of the hot land on the other side of the mountains. He described the ancient people who built ruins on the hilltops and burned bonfires in them every night of the year. The buildings were supposed to be a reflection here below of the order which prevails above. If the earth could be seen from the stars' perspective, he explained, then the buildings with their tiny fires would look to the lofty observer just the way the night sky does to us, only a little smaller.

James's father, whom Frank learned in time to call father, told him stories of the southern cities, of the ports choked with gold and silk and birds in all the colors of the jungle. He told Frank that his parents lived in one of those cities where men live by their wits. They're becoming very rich, James's father said. —When will I go to them? Frank asked. —Ah, not yet, not yet, and James's father sighed. First they must build for you a bedroom with windows that overlook the port, so that every morning you'll wake up to the flapping of sails. A few months later it was: —Not yet! You see, they haven't hired a servant yet to make hot chocolate, which in the south is a delicate business indeed, for it's so hot down there that milk spoils almost before it's squeezed from the cow. You wouldn't want to live without hot chocolate, would you, Frank? Then: —Not yet, Frank. They have to put their business in order before you come. Children cost more to raise down there than they do up here, and your parents won't suffer you to be a poor child. At last James's father said, —How should I know when? They write me only that everything is fine, but slow, and that the weather continues hot. And: —Don't ask me for the letters, Frank. I haven't got them. Paper is made differently in the south; it crumbles to ash after a few minutes in our cold air.

After a year or two Frank stopped asking. When he thought of the mother and father he'd had before, it was with a mixture of mute resentment—if they didn't mind waiting so long to send for him, then he certainly wasn't in a hurry to ask after *them*—and wonder at the green sights they must be seeing, the port's white roofs and the roseate birds whose portraits adorned the covers of his storybooks.

Fifteen years later, Frank met a woman named June at one of the country dances which filled the summer nights with yellow flame, shadows, and the grumble of old automobiles going by. He danced with June; he held her waist and whispered, *If we drive far enough from the fire we'll see the stars. And: Did you know that in the south there used to be an ancient people who built a map of the night sky on hilltops?* —How do you know? June asked, and Frank replied: —It's because my parents live there. They went south when I was very little, and they'll call for me when they're ready for me to come. —Oh! said June. But that's just a figure of speech, isn't it? Frank covered her mouth with his mouth, and it was a long time before he thought to ask, —A figure of speech? —Yes, June said sadly, it's another way of saying dead. It's like dead only more polite. So Frank learned what to anyone else would have been obvious for fifteen years: that his parents had died when he was a child. James's father had told him a story the way a magician produces handkerchiefs from a hat. And Frank, who had been raised to believe that all hats held handkerchiefs, believed them, so tenaciously that James's father had been afraid to show him the secret of the trick, the *Here, look, I keep them knotted in my sleeve, and here I pull them out.* For fifteen years Frank had been victim to a story. June, who understood the magnitude of his mistake, wanted to hold him. But Frank would not be convinced that this was not another trick and that her tugging meant only what it seemed to mean. He wandered from the dim light of the car into the fields which stretched nearly forever in every direction. He walked all night and must have gone in more than one circle, for when dawn came he found himself back at the bonfire, burned down, where the last of the dancers had gone to sleep. He watched them toss like children in their tired dreams and tangle their fingers in one another's hair; he shivered and resolved to learn the truth of everything.

James's parents, it turned out, knew very little. When Frank's mother left them her child, she told them that his father had died of a bad heart. She died not long afterwards, of grief, James's father supposed. His father had been an accountant; his mother's name was Elise. —But what were they like? Frank wanted to know. —Come and see for yourself, James's father said.

Together they went back to the house where, long ago, Frank had been a child.

The rooms were furred with dust, but otherwise untouched. Here were the tables which populated Frank's dimmest dreams, and here, on the walls, maps of the moon which had belonged to his father. In a corner he found the writing desk onto which he'd climbed once to look out the window at the mountains, and through the dusty glass the mountains were as they had always been, blue-purple, jagged, unspeakably remote. Upstairs was the nursery where Frank had learned to sleep, painted the cruel colors of the southern jungle, sharp reds and greens striped with yellow. —It's yours now, James's father said. I've kept it for you, and now it's yours. Frank walked up and down. He found his parents' bedroom, their bed covered with a rough white spread, their dresser and mirror and before the mirror a photograph. —Handsome, aren't they? I think you take after them, Frank. I think you take after them a little. In the photograph Frank's father held his mother by the arm as though leading her somewhere. He wore a deep-brimmed hat which shaded his eyes. His face, thinner than Frank had imagined, was furrowed by a smile. Frank's mother was a beauty. Her narrow shoulders and long hair caught the morning or afternoon sun; she squinted at the camera and grinned, her free arm raised in salutation or warning. —Where is this? Frank asked. The sun burned in squares of glass high overhead; his parents' shadows stretched across a ground of cobblestones. —That? It's the city, where they're from. —They came here? Why? —Oh, there are lots of reasons why people leave the city. Maybe your father wanted quiet for his work, or maybe they were tired of the crowds, or they wanted you to grow up somewhere healthy, not like that cesspool . . . They did talk about going south, Frank. They really did. Frank nodded and went downstairs. When James's father came down he found Frank sitting at the desk, staring out the window. —Sell it, he said. The house explained nothing, changed nothing. He wanted no more to do with its stories, with its lies.

All the same, he made James stop there the day they did not

run away. The house had found no buyers. *The moon saw that place*, people said, which was their way of saying that it was haunted, that it had halfway left this world, and entered the next. Using lengths of plank and nails they found in the cellar, Frank and James boarded up its windows, its front and back doors. When they were done, they stood back to inspect their handiwork. —I'd like to see the moon peek in there now, James said, and Frank nodded. The house belonged to no world at all, anymore: blind and mute, it would tell nothing to anyone. —That ought to hold, Frank said, and they hurried to the bus, which left for the city only once every few days. In Frank's pocket the photograph.

The next night, after James had concluded his business with Rosalyn's father, Frank had his first and only lesson in drawing nature. Together with the three daughters, Frank and James took a ferry to one of the green islands in the jaws of the bay. While the others walked from one gazebo to the next, Frank drew evening meadows and the rise of house-dotted hills. He drew paths that threatened to meet on the far side of wooded ridges, he drew the dark tangle of a grove into which James and Rosalyn disappeared. Frank was the only one surprised when they did not return and could not be found either within the grove or beyond it. The two remaining daughters, embarrassed into silence, led him back across the island to the dock.

—See you Sunday? he said, and Carolyn agreed hesitantly. Evelyn only peered at Frank, as though he had become at once very small and very large, so that it was all she could do to keep him in focus.

BY SUNDAY THE DAUGHTERS WERE GONE, and Frank was working in the laundry, where Mrs. Bellaway had been kind enough to employ him. She was old and had been widowed for so long that it seemed her particular fate was to have become a widow, to stay a widow, and to make sure that the world understood what it was to be a widow. She only hired Frank, she said, because she could see from his face that he was a country boy. Mrs. Bellaway came from the country, too, and understood how easy it was in the city to find oneself penniless, and how hard it was to know what to do next. Frank's poverty, of course, was the doing of another country boy: when James left, he took Frank's savings. *You won't need money as long as you can draw*, he wrote Frank on the stationery of a hotel in a distant city. *Good luck with the other two.*

The same day Charles received a long letter from Rosalyn. He would never afterwards reveal what she wrote, but the guests in the parlor saw the hunchback raise the letter over his head as though to ward off some misfortune from above; holding it so, he ran out of the boardinghouse. His eyes still on the letter, he didn't see the bucket and mop he'd left on the front steps; he stepped in the one, tripped over the other, and landed on the sidewalk with his leg in an untenable position. Charles went home to mend, and his daughters left to care for him. A few weeks later Mrs. Bellaway let Frank know that the hunchback had retired from the boardinghouse business, and had taken his daughters with him, lest they elope with the transients who remained.

Mrs. Bellaway let Frank keep the garret, but having no use for pictures, least of all pictures of herself, she told him that he would have to earn his keep some other way. The first night after James and Rosalyn's elopement, he toyed with the botanist's tools until it was nearly light, then dozed for an hour or two, and dreamed of dried flowers taking on the scorched colors of the country at midsummer. The next morning he went to work on the boarders' clothes.

The season turned, and the judges came to take the place of the transients. They ate early in the bright and stuffy dining room, and vanished immediately afterwards into the sound of doors firmly closed and the shuffling of pages. Frank never saw a single judge, but he acquired an intimate knowledge of their robes: he plunged the black gowns into cold water with a little soap and no bleach, and their white shirts into hot water, using more soap and a good deal of bleach, which Mrs. Bellaway got for free from a nephew who worked in a bleach factory, and so could afford to use generously. Mrs. Bellaway he saw often enough to be interested by her face and then to understand it, to draw her long jaw

and flat skull, her deep eyes and narrow nose and her upper lip
with its fine bleached hairs; he understood her face, grew sick of
it, and gradually ceased to notice it altogether. He learned the
names of the rest of the boardinghouse staff: the cook Alonso
who was always tired and played an instrument which Frank
thought was a mandolin; Jerome the night porter and Gerald the
day porter, old insomniacs who were both awake at all hours in
front of the radio. The maid, named Monique or Monica, liked
Frank at the beginning, but not so much afterwards, when she fell
in love with a court reporter who came to Bellaway's on business.

At first Mrs. Bellaway gave Frank Wednesday evenings off;
when she saw that he was a capable worker she gave him Sunday
afternoons as well. Frank went walking then, sketchbook pressed
between elbow and rib. What he had seen since his arrival was
only the smallest fraction of the city. Now, leaving behind the
monuments, the Cathedral Square, and the avenues which radi-
ated out from it like the spokes of an enormous wheel, he came to
a part of the city where the streets had trees, and a part where they
had once had trees but didn't anymore and weren't about to; to a
part of the city where silvered-glass windows made the houses
impossible to look at in the sun, and a part where the buildings,
made of violet brick and soot, were decrepit and morose no matter when you looked at them. At night he returned to the garret
and sketched what he had seen. His landscapes were clearer than
they had been before, if less populous; but they brought him little comfort. Now and then he thought he heard James's footsteps
in the hall, or Rosalyn's characteristic, half-contented sigh; he
went out to look and found that it was only one of the maids
shaking out her umbrella after a day in the country. Frank closed

his door again, paced, peered out the window to see whether the light was on in the yellow room.

One Sunday, in an interval between fall rains, Frank at last set out for the street in the photograph, which he had located on a map with the help of the Great Evan, the magician he'd met at Bellaway's. He didn't know what he expected to find there, or rather he expected to find nothing—but it was a nothing he needed to see for himself. Having taken in the absence of two figures in an otherwise empty street, along with all that meant, he would be free, he thought, from the last of the questions which had troubled him ever since he learned what was meant by *going south*. But he must have turned his map the wrong way, or else the magician had given him bad directions. At the end of an afternoon he found himself in a distant part of the city where the houses were made of old wood, canvas, and sheets of tin, and the air smelled like burning garbage. Bottles rattled like knives at the end of blind alleys.

He was about to turn back when he caught sight of a corpse in the road and a woman with a camera. The corpse, a man, wore a black coat; he lay on his face with his arms stretched in front of him, palms down. The woman circled the body, crouched, then stood, turned the camera on its side, took a step back, and crouched again. Frank walked closer, just to have a look. When he was ten or fifteen feet away, the photographer called, —Stay back, will you?

—What is it?

—Crime scene.

He could see only half her face behind the camera's viewfinder: a moon-hued oval, with almond eyes that blinked in the dusty light, as though she had spent her formative years away from the sun. Were it not for her precise, graceful animation, she might herself have been a corpse. And Frank wondered whether, as the city was so large that not all of it could be in use at the same time, some parts might not have been given over to the dead. Who could say, under the circumstances, that they would not enjoy taking one another's pictures?

The photographer's shoulders curved forward as she fished a filter from her vest, and a trail of black hair swept across her back.

—I think I know you, Frank said.

—I doubt it.

—I can see your window from my window. Not—he blushed—that I look.

—Oh?

—You live across from Bellaway's. That's where I live, at least, where I . . . Frank fumbled for an impressive way to describe his situation. —Where I'm staying now.

—All right, we're neighbors. The photographer knelt to get a closer look at the corpse's shoes.

—I'm Frank.

—Prudence.

—That's an unusual name.

She appeared not to have heard him. After she'd taken a picture of the hat of the deceased, however, she said, —My father named us all for virtues. I was the youngest, and by the time I was born, it was the only one left. Can you step back? There might be footprints.

Without meaning to, Frank had got close to the body again. He retreated to what he hoped was a safe distance. Footprints? The

mud all around the corpse was trampled as though by a herd of cattle; you could no more tell one footprint from another in that jumble than you would, by inspecting a grain of sand, be able to say the shape of the stone from which it had come.

—Are you a police officer?

Prudence glared at him over the camera's viewfinder. —I'm a photographer.

—Ah.

—Why, what do you do?

—I work in the laundry at Mrs. Bellaway's. And I draw.

—For money?

—No.

—Ah.

The police arrived. They rolled the corpse onto its back. It wore the clothes of a lawyer or a banker, although the officers spoke of the deceased in connection with a man named Eyeless and a plot to smuggle books, birds, and snakes in from the unruly country to the east. One detective mentioned aliases. Another said cyanide. The dead man's face was ordinary and a bit dour, a thin-lipped square-foreheaded face like a dozen others Frank had drawn one afternoon in the business district. —Thanks, ma'am, the officers said, when Prudence handed them the rolls of film. No one asked Frank who he was; they didn't seem to care whether he was there or not.

It was dark by the time they'd finished, and Bellaway's was too far away to walk; so, as a kindness, Prudence offered Frank a ride home in her small, bottle-green car. Its headlights, loose in their sockets, shook slightly as they drove, so that the road seemed always to curve, and the city, for a few minutes, revealed an older, serpentine version of itself.

—Are there a lot of dead people? Frank asked.

—What?

—To photograph, I mean.

—Oh, yes, hundreds. Thousands on a bad night. You can hardly see the street for all the bodies piled up in it.

—Really?

—No.

—I'm sorry. It's just that I don't know the city very well, yet.

—Where are you from? Prudence asked.

He told her the name of the place. —It's far away, he explained, and not very big. And you?

—I'm from here. Prudence pointed toward a distant hill, a part of the city Frank had never visited.

She stopped at a café near Mrs. Bellaway's. —I need coffee, always, after I go out. Do you want some?

Prudence told Frank that she had been a police photographer for seven years, that she had by her count taken pictures of three thousand six hundred and eighty-two corpses, of all ages and all sorts, in all parts of the city. There were more murders now than there had been before. But the police force is also increasing, she said, so don't worry. She told him how she had begun her career as a portrait photographer, but made no money at it because she hated to take pictures in a hurry. Sometimes her subjects would walk out of the studio before she'd exposed a single frame of film, although, if they waited, they generally found that she'd captured something in them which faster ways of seeing could not grasp. Corpses were, in this sense, her ideal subjects. Prudence had a knack for police work. She could capture the entire death in fewer images than any other photographer on the force. It was a matter of framing, she said: everything was clear if you got the right bit of background. A telltale scrap of paper, a mailbox, a theater marquee. The experts in the lab had told her, more than once, that her pictures could make a dead man speak. —That's how they speak, you know, she said matter-of-factly. —In pictures.

She stood up. —Well, I'm bushed, you?

—Can I . . . Can I come with you?

—What, now?

—When you, when you photograph them.

—Want to learn the trade, huh? Prudence laughed. Well, come, if you want. I'm glad of the company. She wrote her number on a page torn from the book she had almost finished reading, a novel in which cars figured prominently.

That night Frank stayed up late, working at the table under the electric lamp. He drew the corpse's face from memory and compared it to the live faces he had drawn; he found no difference between the two. Strange city, he thought, and rested his head in his hands. Dawn found him there, his eyes closed, recalling the faces of the living and of the dead.

When he was a very small child—before his proper memories began, so that afterwards he was never sure whether he remembered events themselves, or only memories of those events— Frank's father had told him a story about how the city was founded on a giant's grave. Where the giant came from none of those who built the city knew; they found him there at the end of their journey, at the ocean's edge, an enormous corpse lying face up on the shore with one arm extended in the direction of the hills and the other arm flung toward the sea. In the cupped palm of his landward hand, birds had made their nests; in the hand which lay just beneath the low-tide mark, crabs had taken their meals, so that the fingers were reduced to bones. When the founders of the city arrived at the giant's corpse they stopped, not knowing what to make of such a body. This is a sign that we are indeed very small, said the fainthearted among them. We should not dream of building a city, for what would anything we could build be in comparison with a giant? Others thought that the giant's corpse was a sign they must triumph. If they lived where so large a creature had fallen, did it not mean that within their little frames there was some spark to outdo nature's marvels? A third faction held that the body was a sign their city would fail, but in failing would leave the world a wonder such as it had never seen before. Voices spoke for the city and voices spoke against it. They noted the smell given off by the corpse each time the wind blew from the ocean, and how they would have to live among the droppings of the carrion birds. Torn between prudes and visionaries, the explorers foundered. Finally, it was decided that the only way to appease both sides would be to bury the giant. But the body stretched three miles up and down the coast; its head was the size of a hill and each of its feet a peak; its legs from a distance might have been mistaken for the arms of a mountain stretching down toward the water. Working in the noisome shade of the giant's landward side, pelted day and night by the dung of birds, the founders dug. They prepared a trench three miles long and half again as wide; it was as deep as the giant's body was thick, or a little deeper. With superhuman effort, letting the tide float the body along, they pulled it into the trench. The corpse rolled on its side and got stuck, so that part of the body protruded above the pit's rim. The founders couldn't countenance burying the giant again; they filled in what they could of the grave and built their city around the rest. The head became a cathedral, and the arm a fortification; a bony finger pointing skywards served them as a spire. After centuries of use, the buildings of bone fell into ruin along with the rest of the old city. A new cathedral was built across the river, and the fortifications became home to a warren of shacks nested in the fissures of the wall. The rain ate away the spire, which grew lighter and lighter; just before it broke off, strange patterns appeared in its exterior, which some called writing, though others said they were pictures of the world as it had been when giants lived there. After three or four generations more, the city's inhabitants forgot about the giant. This bump in the earth? they would have said, if anyone had asked them. —Why, it's just a lump of stone, a wrinkle in the earth's skin. And the long seawall where the beggars have their huts? Well, the craft of the ancients was in some ways quite advanced. We don't know what they made the wall of, but we like it there because it keeps the water out. The yellowed stump, etched with whorls and lines, which reaches still toward the stars? It's an old temple; that's how they were built, with thick walls and an interior no wider than a well, because in those days people still believed that the gods were curious about individuals, and so preferred to see mortals one at a time. So each part of the giant was explained away. And along with the great corpse the city's inhabitants forgot a number of other, less important things: the old belief that insects were hatched from sea foam, and the custom of wearing oilskin hats. Even precious things slipped from their minds, like the way they had of loving one another silently, which in the old days brought a hush to the city in early spring and again at midsummer, when blue-green light washed the city almost until morning. Nor should it be surprising that these things were lost, for if people are capable of forgetting a giant three miles long, what can they not put out of their minds?

It was as though an important relic had been passed into Frank's custody. For weeks he made it his duty to think constantly of the giant. Days, when the afternoon light yellowed the plains, he thought of the giant's yellow bones, of its sky-pointing finger. In the summer heat, which did not die until late in the evening, he thought of those parts of the giant submerged in the cool earth, the legs and unimaginably vast rib cage, the buried eye socket and the buried hand. At night before Frank fell asleep he instructed himself to dream of the giant, and indeed, many nights, he fell asleep to thoughts of the living giant, who took a mile in a step and left footprints deep as lakes and long as towns. Slowly, however, Frank's vigil broke into islets of giant-thought in a sea of other things: what it would be like to live on the other side of the mountains, and whether he could have soup for dinner, and a thousand smaller but more immediate wonders. Now and then he'd recall a bit of the giant, guiltily: a bone so long he couldn't see either end of it, or the sharp ridges of an enormous tooth. Soon even these fragments slipped away; when Frank heard the word *giant* or *bones* he blushed a little, as though remembering a time when he'd been caught playing with dolls.

Much later, when he gave up hope that his parents would send for him, Frank wondered whether it wasn't in some way his fault, whether he shouldn't have been thinking of the giant all along.

·   ·   ·

He called Prudence as soon as his work in the laundry was done, and in no time her bottle-green car stopped outside Mrs. Bellaway's, waiting to take Frank to see the murdered. It was as if the giant's corpse had been replaced by a thousand smaller bodies: a financier had his throat cut behind the dog track; a longshoreman bumped against the pier; a housepainter hung from the chandelier of a half-finished hotel. Two men in matching coats had shot each other in a dispute over some bauble, broken now, which gleamed dimly at the mouth of a gutter. The police found corpses curled like sleeping children in the back seats of cars, in movie theaters and the upper balcony of the New Opera House, in the thickets of the arboretum, slumped over the rail of the riverside promenade. It was nearly morning by the time Prudence handed the last roll of film to the last investigating officer and returned, wearily, to the car. The air smelled of soil. There must be a park somewhere nearby, Frank thought, but he could see nothing of the sort, only factories lit red and blue intermittently by the police cars. —Well? asked Prudence. What do you think?

—It looks like hard work, Frank said.

—Oh, it's not so bad. All I have to do is take the pictures, and the police do the rest.

—They must be very good.

—Apparently there's no one like them anywhere.

Then, as though she found the topic distasteful, Prudence said, —Want to get some coffee?

They stopped in a café by the railroad station, the sort of place where time itself seems to have been held up by an unexpected delay somewhere farther down the line. Old men dozed at the counter or studied the racing form over a long-cold cup of tea;

day laborers from outlying towns washed down their morning egg with their morning beer. Prudence had begun some story in the car which Frank was too tired to follow; instead, he'd watched the sky turn blue and fill the city with a hollow light, as though everything had become its own shadow. —And that, Prudence concluded, is why I'll never fall in love again.

—What? Frank blushed. —Sorry. It's late . . .

Prudence stirred her coffee. Outside, a bell rang once, and again, announcing the morning.

—What do you think of this camera? she asked.

It looked small, and old, but Frank hesitated to say so, in the first place because his experience with cameras was limited, and in the second because a small camera might narrow things down, which would make it suitable for police work. —It's very nice, he said.

—It's lousy. I should have bought a new one years ago.

—Why don't you, then?

Instead of answering, Prudence told Frank how, when she was a girl, she had been to see a palmist, an old man whose perpetual misery in the face of growing financial ease had earned him a reputation as a true visionary. He took one look at Prudence's hand and groaned. —You're clever, and what a misfortune! For you won't fall in love until you find someone you can't fool. Prudence admitted that she had been young enough to take the prediction as a challenge. She found that foolish men were easy to fool, and clever ones not much harder, if only because none of them could guess . . .

—What?

—No, it's not important.

—Oh.

—That is . . . Prudence laughed and drank her coffee down. Frank got the impression that, behind the mug she held to her mouth with both hands, she was smiling more broadly still. —Let's go, she said, and pulled Frank outside. The morning smelled of bread. The sun had cleared the clock tower, and the streetcars came by to claim the day's workers; from silence everything had turned to commotion. Silver rails shone in the middle of the street; they ran around a corner into what seemed to Frank an indefinite distance.

Work took the photographer to all parts of the city, and in particular to the dangerous ones: the hills where the fog rarely lifted, and almost anything could be done unseen, and the city's center, behind the theaters, where derelicts decked themselves out in the velvet doublets and horned caps discarded by the costumers. One night as they drove from the city's last working windmill to the dead earth where its last winery had succumbed to its last disease of plants, Frank asked Prudence if she knew the whole city. —Ha! she replied. I'd have to be a hundred and nineteen years old. She explained that there was a story, told mostly to children, about nine old men who walked around with the entire city in their heads. They might have any profession, be rich or poor, disfigured, blind, or mute, but each was required to be a hundred and nineteen years old, for, the story went, that was how long it took to walk the length of each and every street in the city. The Mayor and the City Council were supposed to seek these nine men out each time they made an important decision, but, without knowing whom to look for, they were reduced to stopping toothless old men on street corners and asking them whether or not it would be right to build a new arena, or to tear down the aqueduct—with the result that they got a lot of senile and incoherent advice, and followed it meticulously, contributing further to the city's disarray. Frank nodded, and Prudence had to remind him that it *was* only a story; she supposed that plans for each district could be found somewhere in the archives of the Planning Commission.

What was true, and what was only a story? The dead speak in pictures, Prudence said, and Frank wanted to believe her. He watched the corpses carefully. Sometimes he thought he could see their deaths in their faces: a tightness of the lips, a way the eyes had of being open too far, or closed too loosely; and sometimes he couldn't see anything. All the same, Frank tried to teach himself to draw the dead. He had no interest in detective work. Unlike the Analysis division of the police department, he did not care to know why the faces ringed in chalk and revolving lights had died, and not the other faces which still walked about the city, nodding good morning, and selling him paper sacks of fruit. Frank suspected that this was the business of photographs, which, unlike drawings, were admissible as evidence in court: they invited the dead to speak on legal matters, questions of guilt and fault. A drawing, he reasoned, was different: animating the corpse by means of ink and imagination, he ought to be able to make it speak on whatever subject he chose; there was no secret he could not ask it to tell. He didn't say so to Prudence, of course, but he thought such sketches might be worth even more than her photographs. For, despite all the corpses he'd seen, Frank believed that there must be something more to life than its end.

Even murder, when seen properly, was of less interest than what had come before, whatever story had been interrupted.

So, in his sketchbook, the catalogue of houses gave way to an inventory of cadavers: faces punctuated with bullet holes or underscored by the dark dash of a garrote; tongues thick with poison and eyes discolored by river water. He followed Prudence as she circled the bodies, and tried to sketch from the points where she took her pictures. Then, hoping that intuition would prove a better guide, he struck out toward angles of his own: head-on views of porkpie hats, shoes in profile. It was no use. Whether because he had no talent for the work, or because the ectoplasm of dead souls adhered only to photographic paper, Frank's sketches were mute. And when, considering that the city's deceased might be reluctant to tell their secrets to a provincial, he tried to conceive of his own dead faces, Frank found that the white rectangle of the page had become like a boarded-up window behind which he could imagine only empty rooms.

BY THE END OF FALL, WHEN THE UNPAVED streets had turned to mud and the gutters overflowed with water-worn leaves, Frank gave up trying to draw the dead. He threw some of his sketches on the bonfire which burned all through the week in Cathedral Square, commemorating the end of a harvest season that had long ago ceased to have any importance for the citizens; the rest of the drawings he planned to throw away, and forgot about, instead. Like a contracting elastic band, his thinking returned to its original shape. He watched Prudence as she circled the bodies, and admired the arc of her hip, her slender fingers, and the sweep of her hair as she brushed it away from her eyes. One night when her picture-taking had gone particularly well, and the killed seemed to give up the names of their killers even before the film was developed, Frank took advantage of her elation to ask her to sit for him.

Prudence looked at him, incredulous.
—You have a kid?

—No, for a portrait, so I can draw you.

She smiled. —A portrait? I thought those were just for the museums. She told him how, when she was a girl, she'd gone to the galleries of the old Historical Society, where the painted eyes of long-dead mayors not only followed passersby but wept to see them go; droplets of water rolled from the oil paint and discolored the marble floor. For centuries the city's exorcists, psychologists, and historians of art had maintained that paintings felt loss even more acutely than living men, for they were less able to move about and find things again. Then an earthquake cracked the vault of the gallery; the workmen sent to repair the damage found pairs of tiny holes in the roof, above where the portraits hung. Nothing was resolved: the art historians and psychologists continued to debate whether the holes had been drilled there by some prankster, or whether they constituted a part of the museum's original design.

Frank blushed; it seemed that everything in the city belonged to one tradition or another, so that as a newcomer he was bound to do everything wrong.

—Well, but tell me, Prudence said, what should I wear?

One portrait became many; for months Prudence sat every Sunday afternoon in Frank's room. It wasn't that she was beautiful but that she was never still, so that it was impossible to say what she would look like at rest, in one place, from one angle. Even when Frank asked her please not to move, she would turn her head slightly from side to side, lean back in her chair, then lean forward again. His portraits were all blurred; there were never fewer than three Prudences on the page, each of them indistinct but distinctly different from the other two. Frank did not tire of trying to condense these three into a single, perfect image.

While she sat, Prudence told him how she had been a girl in the city, and gone to school with the daughters of senators and ecclesiasts. They learned to count, to jump rope, and to find patterns in past events; they learned that the city was a giant machine with senators and ecclesiasts for gears and rods. The girls learned that their role was akin to that of the night janitor in the machine room: able neither to fix the machine nor to stop it, but only, if she learned her job well, to squeeze a drop or two of oil into the works. Prudence had never resigned herself to that, and so, when her school friends went off to drink, dance, and marry, she enrolled in the Quadrilateral University, which was so old, and so well loved, that its courtyards were choked with the statues of benefactors, who stood so close to one another that they seemed to embrace, to strike one another's cheeks, or to rub noses. The first thing one learned as a student there was how to find one's way between them without getting lost. Prudence studied in the renowned departments of theology and economics. She disputed with her peers by day, and by night labored over equations which, if done correctly, would prove the asymptotic rise of mankind toward a distant divinity. After graduation she found that there was little call for her proofs, which in any case remained unfinished. Prudence wondered whether she wouldn't have done better to follow her childhood friends into the arms of the city's great men; but a few visits to their houses, where overfed children climbed the backs of overstuffed chairs, and set fire to things in corners, convinced her that she was better off as she was. She spent a year teaching history to the blind, and then, at the end of her purse, she went to see her uncle, who worked in the police department. —And you? Prudence asked.

—Me?

—What was it like in the country?

—It was nothing special.

—Tell me something at least. Where did you live?

—In a house.

—And you call yourself an artist! Which, strictly speaking, wasn't true, but Frank let it pass. —What was it like?

—I had a bedroom with flowers on the walls. And a window with a view of the mountains. They're really very high, the mountains, but so far away that you can hardly tell.

—Why did you leave?

—Don't move for a second. Frank concentrated on the line of her shoulders, but Prudence would not be distracted.

—Tell me.

Faltering at first, not quite able to find the right words nor to give up and use the wrong ones, Frank told her how he had left the house where he had been a child, and how he had left it again fifteen years later.

—You never knew your real parents? Prudence asked.

—No, I mean yes, I knew them.

—What were they like?

Frank bit the end of his brush. If he thought about it delicately, and did not, so to speak, look directly at it, but allowed it to float in the corner of his mind's eye, he could see his father's face, his rumpled hair, his eyes ringed with disappointment.

—My father had a map of the moon, with all the craters and seas labeled, he said.

I'm going to find something up there, something no one's ever seen. Had he been an astronomer? But James's father said he was an accountant. *They're going to write my name on that map, one day.* What was true, and what was only a story?

—I don't think he was very happy, Frank said.

—How did he die?

—He went out to look at the moon one night . . . I don't know. *Look carefully. Tell me what you see through the telescope. Is that all? I know all of those already.*

—And your mother?

—I don't remember.

—What did she look like?

—I'll show you. Frank left his easel and rummaged about in the suitcase he'd brought with him from the country. He threw knots of shirts and socks onto the bed, then an extra pair of shoes, a woolen scarf he'd had occasion to use but forgotten about, the stub of his bus ticket, a handful of pebbles he'd picked up on a path somewhere in the city, enchanted by how they looked in the evening light. By day they were ordinary pebbles. —I have a photo somewhere.

But it was gone. Frank unfolded everything, turned the bag upside-down and shook it, stuck his head under the bed, and came up frowning. —I don't know what happened to it. Distracted, he forgot his easel and the portrait which he'd left just on the cusp of some definition; he paced back and forth, looked through the botanist's old supplies, and even peered out the window as though he expected to see the picture hanging from a tree in the courtyard. —It's gone.

—You should try the Found Objects Bureau, Prudence said.

—The what?

She explained: So many things turned up in the city that the police department had taken charge of classifying them and returning them to their proper owners. In the early days of the Bureau, the lost things had been mostly pocketbooks, wallets, umbrellas, rings, keys, hats, gloves, scarves, and the like: the portable manifestations of the citizens' public identities. But as soon as the police department took charge of returning them, it became aware that they were the least of what turned up in the storm drains and bus depots, the train station and the coat checks of the city's museums. There were suitcases full of wigs, pages of fine handwriting, baby bottles half-full of yellow milk, false teeth and long-stemmed pipes, undergarments, prophylactics, letters, ointments, diaries, a collection of increasingly private objects which had to be categorized and made available to their owners. As soon as the categories existed and shelf space had been allotted for them, the shelves had to be filled; the Bureau's agents took to searching wastebaskets and lurking behind private stairways, hoping to catch a pacifier or a matchbook as soon as it was dropped, for the city's police—who knew it better than Prudence?—were of the philosophy that their citizens would be better served by thoroughness than by benevolence. The agents were there when a family left its home, waiting to collect whatever had been left behind; they requested a budget from the commissioner of police in order to buy up everything that had been left in pawnshops: harps and trousers, cuff links and raincoats. When the warehouses were full with the paraphernalia of the city's lost lives, the agents shifted their attention to the collection of intangibles. The Bureau became a repository for ambitions, hypotheses, cravings, resolutions, intuitions, and designs, all recorded as numbered entries in numbered notebooks, waiting for their owners to come and reclaim them. As most citizens were hardly aware that such things, once lost, could be found again, the notebooks gathered dust even as they grew in number. The Bureau was in a state of perpetual crisis as to where its next annex would be built. There are neighborhoods, Prudence said, where every third house belongs to them. So they'll certainly have found your photo, she concluded. They find everything.

—That's just a story, isn't it? Frank asked.

—No, it's real enough. Do you want to go?

Frank looked back at the picture on the easel. He thought he could see how, if he added only a few lines, he might, once and for all, have a likeness of Prudence's face.

—Don't worry about it, he said. After all, it's just a photograph.

—Just a photograph? Prudence laughed, and Frank reassured her that he meant no slight to her profession.

—Sit still for a minute, he said.

Another stroke ought to fix the curve of her cheek—but it came out too thick and too dark, as though she were tugging her head free of some clinging shadow. He tried to correct it, but the picture was already ruined, and each added stroke only made it worse. —I give up, he said. Do you want to go out?

They went to a nightclub in the part of the city where the buildings were made of iron, where a singer sang about the aching specificity of her native streets to the lullaby tunes of the accompanist. Prudence was a dancer without equal; her motion matched itself to the music until it wasn't clear which of the two, music or motion, was the cause and which the effect. Even the noctambules were in bed by the time they left the club, arm in arm; apart from

the rumble of night buses and taxis, the city was still. At Bellaway's door Prudence took Frank's hands in her own, and, as
though still executing the steps of a dance, pulled herself up on
tiptoes, so that her lips were level with his. For a moment Frank
could see which way this dance went: he kissed her, and they remained in that pose, Prudence straining a little not to fall back
down, until the traffic's diminuendo faded out altogether.

—I love the quiet, Prudence said. It's the only time the city
seems alive. Don't you think?

—I . . .

—Don't say anything, then.

She kissed him again, curtsied, and was gone.

That night Frank dreamed he had got lost in an arcade decorated with an intricate frieze, on which mayors and duodeca-
genarians, corpses and cameras, widows and windows told him
all they knew. He woke, perfectly happy, to the sound of the winter rain.

A particularly insoluble crime was committed in the part of the
city where the houses seemed to be made of mud, and in place of
doors the doorways made do with flags and other brightly colored scraps of cloth. —Third one tonight, the policeman said
when Prudence arrived. —Must be the weather. The rain had
continued without relief since morning. —Must be the season.

—Can you shine your light over here, officer? I want to get a
picture of this puddle. Prudence went to work, and Frank, who
had already seen that there was nothing special about the corpse,
wandered off. He followed one street and then another, looking
back often to make sure that he could still see the colored lights

of the police cars. He stopped at the end of the third street, where a turn would have taken him into the unrelieved darkness of the neighborhood. Frank didn't want to get lost, but he wasn't ready to go back, so he stood at the end of the street and waited.

The clouds parted; in the middle of the road, three children appeared, a girl and two boys. The children must have been there all along, Frank thought; but they were dressed in black, their hands and faces covered in mud, so they were visible only by moonlight. They moved solemnly about; the girl sat cross-legged in the middle of the street, and the boys took up positions before her. The first boy sang,

Guilty moon, guilty moon,
Hang you from a wooden spoon,
Hang the spoon upon a star,
Hang the star above your head,
Close the blinds, and go to bed.

When he was done, the second boy sang a similar rhyme; then it was the girl's turn. She sang so softly that Frank couldn't make out the words. He stepped closer. *Hang your heart*, she sang, then Frank slipped and fell on his knees.

—Hey! one of the boys called out.

The children all looked at him. Frank stood up. His pants were splashed with mud, and when he tried to brush them off, his muddy hands only made things worse. The children laughed and ran off down the street, their black sleeves flapping like small wings.

Prudence was waiting for him by the police car. —Where were you? she asked. You have to be careful in this neighborhood. It's dangerous.

—I know, Frank said. When he looked up, it was raining again and the moon was gone.

He tried to find the lunar children again. The children he saw, however, were all of the ordinary sort; their games were familiar, terrestrial, and more or less innocent. It was while he was looking that he noticed the posters on the streets, in the supermarkets, pasted to lampposts and tacked to trees, which announced that people were missing. Have you seen Saul, 13, wearing a blue-and-yellow shirt and carrying a green bag with a picture of a dog on it? Last seen in October on such-and-such a street corner. Looking for Mona, beloved wife, missing since she went out for groceries on the first day of the year. The posters were everywhere; Frank wondered why he hadn't seen them before. At first he stopped to read them only on his way from one place to another; but the descriptions fascinated him. Each one corresponded to the life of a citizen who had disappeared; together, they constituted the seeds of another city, at once here in front of him and terribly far away.

Frank slept badly. Late at night, when Prudence had gone home, he wandered from sign to sign, reading the names of the missing. When his legs grew tired he lay on his back in a vacant lot, listening to the insects trill in their piles of rubble, and watched the moon. He thought sometimes of the posters, and sometimes of Prudence's face, which blurred in his memory as it had in his portraits; he thought of the city and the house and the lost photograph. There was something about it all that he could not explain. The city seemed to expand and contract in ripples around him, as though he were a stone that had been cast onto its surface, to sink into the still waters below. As for the moon, it told him nothing; it neither grew nor shrank nor appeared to move, but stayed resolutely in its corner of the sky, fading in and out of sight with the coming and going of the day and the clouds at night.

During the day Frank worked at Mrs. Bellaway's, washing the judges' robes. He divided his nights between the murdered, the missing, and the moon. On Sundays he accumulated a portfolio of Prudence in ink and watercolor, in oil and chalk and charcoal. No matter what materials he used, he could not hold her still, even in his eye, even for a moment.

Only once did he think he'd seen her motionless. It happened after the equinox, when the lengthening days kept the garret alive with golden light. Frank had been trying to draw Prudence since midafternoon, with no more success than he usually had; in fact, a little less than usual because he was using pastels which crumbled when he applied them to the rough paper he'd chosen, leaving granular trails like the footprints of children running over wet sand. Prudence told Frank how she wished, sometimes, that she had never become a photographer, never gone to work for the police. —It gets so that all you can see is crime, she said. Even when I'm not working, I see it in people's faces. I see what they'll look like, murdered, the way you can imagine how someone will look when they're old.

All the same, Prudence feared that the detectives were dissatisfied with her work. At first, when she gave them her rolls of film, they cradled the plastic cylinders as though they were the eggs of rare birds. Now they shoved the film into their trench coats unceremoniously, with hardly a word of thanks, or thanked her the way she imagined they thanked their informers, with a mixture of deference and contempt. Was it because she'd lost her knack? But the pictures seemed just as telling to her as they had before, even if she chose certain angles now more out of habit than from any inspiration. Or was it because . . . no, she couldn't say it. No, she'd say it: was it because she'd made a mistake? Had her pictures fingered some innocent whose innocence was revealed too late, and were the police in trouble for it, and if so, why didn't they tell her? Perhaps, for some reason known only to themselves, they wanted her to make mistakes, perhaps all along she had made nothing but mistakes and the police had led her on, telling her how talented she was and laughing to themselves all the while.

Frank reassured her that the police would never do such a thing, certainly, and that if they did, it was their own fault and none of hers.

The conversation got around to the suitors Prudence had entertained as a girl, and how each one had come to grief, undone by her desire to trick them in one way or another. The fools she'd fooled with wit, and the clever ones with silence; those in between she put off with too much flattery or too little, with brashness or prudishness. Everyone could be tricked somehow. All that had ended years ago, she said, after she fell in love with a professor of economics at the Quadrilateral University. He was much older than she, and renowned for his complex theories of want. He loved her because back then she was quite a beauty—she looked at the floor, and Frank lost track of her face once again—and because she was a good student, who seemed to grasp his theorems intuitively. They were lovers for years. He spoke of having her lecture at the university, and of the books they'd write together. On him Prudence played the cruelest trick of all. For her final project, she wrote a paper exposing a small flaw at the heart of his work, which rendered all his theorems, if not invalid, at least inapplicable to any possible world. The paper made quite a sensation in academic circles, and ended her lover's career. After it was circulated, he called Prudence into his office. —I've told the faculty how you seduced me, he said. I very much doubt you'll find work at this university, or at any other.

He gave her a camera, a simple machine, practically a toy. —You'll need a hobby when you're settled down, he said, and I thought, as you have such sharp eyes . . . Prudence took the camera—what else could she do? he put it in her hand, and closed her fingers on it—and left. She did not attend the university's graduation; by then she had started her job teaching history to the blind. At least they would not know to envy her eyes, she reasoned, having none of their own. When, a year later, she found that she'd been wrong about that, she went to see her uncle on the police force. —What can you do? he asked, and Prudence joked, —I have a camera.

By then the light had failed altogether, or nearly so; even the brightest reds—which were in any case useless for Prudence's pale skin—could hardly be seen on the blue-gray page. Rather than turn on the electric lamp, Frank let the pastels drop and sat down opposite Prudence at the botanist's table.

—That's what I get for playing tricks. Prudence smiled bitterly.

—But it wasn't your fault.

—All the same, I haven't had a lover since. And I don't want one, either.

—Oh? Frank blushed and, to hide his embarrassment, opened one of the botanist's albums. The names of plants and flowers had been written carefully in ink, but the pages were empty of specimens dried or drawn. The other pages in the album were the same.

—How do you know I wouldn't trick you, too? Prudence asked.

—Would you?

Frank could see only the shine of her hair in the moonlight.

—I'm not sure I would, she said. And then: —Would you go away with me?

—Away to where?

—Anywhere, really. It doesn't matter. Would you go?

—Yes.

For a moment, there, although he could hardly see her, it seemed to him that Prudence was perfectly still.

Weeks later there was a great storm; the next morning parts of the city were gone. He heard the news from Mrs. Bellaway; she found him in the laundry in the middle of the afternoon, when he was done with the black robes and had just put the linen in a tub of hot water to soak. —Did you hear, she wailed, did you hear what happened?

—No.

—You know there was a storm?

—I heard it. Frank had woken up in the middle of the night to the sound of rain; he looked out the window but could see nothing at all for the water and the clouds. The power must have gone out, because even his electric clock was dark. He went back to sleep, and the next morning the view was as it had been before, with clouds moving very quickly across the sky.

—Houses, entire houses, were washed away. Mrs. Bellaway tottered, and steadied herself against the mangle.

—Away to where?

—That's just it! she shouted. No one knows to where!

—That's impossible. Houses don't do that.

—Well, they did it last night. An entire street vanished. No one saw it go. The neighbors were all visiting friends, and when they came back the next morning, the street was gone, and everyone in it, too.

—That's too bad.

—My nephews! Lived on that street! Mrs. Bellaway coughed.

—Oh dear. Frank offered her a wet handkerchief.

—My nephew John, who works in the bleach factory, and my nephew Lawrence, who makes kites for the blind.

—I'm sorry.

Mrs. Bellaway released her hold on the mangle. —Don't be sorry. Just don't waste the bleach, now, do you hear?

Frank called Prudence as soon as he was done with work. —Did you hear about the street that disappeared?

—What street, she said, and Frank explained.

—Oh. Well, those houses just wash away sometimes. Serves them right for not living in stone houses, or at the very least houses made of wood.

—But the people? People don't wash away. The police haven't called you about this?

—It's a big city, Frank. If they've been murdered, they'll turn up, and if not, why worry about them?

—I suppose. Frank carried the phone to the windowsill. He could see Prudence in her yellow room, arranging what looked like flowers. —Maybe people will put up posters.

—Posters?

—You know, the ones you put up when you're looking for someone.

—I've never . . . Prudence hesitated.

—You haven't seen them?

—I'm not a hundred and nineteen.

—Tonight, said Frank, why don't you come out with me?

It was past midnight when she knocked on his door, her camera hanging as always from her shoulder. Fog filled the streets, hiding the buildings and softening the sounds of the night-watchmen and streetwalkers, the newspaper deliverymen and lamplighters and the children who fished for change in the neaping storm drains, the city's nighttime population. Like a melancholic tour guide, Frank led Prudence to one poster and another, introducing each missing person with a wave of his hand, saying, —This one is Mona. And —Over here we have Saul. Prudence said nothing. After the first lot of posters she took his hand; sometime in the night, damp and chilled by the fog, she slid her shoulder against his arm and held her side to his side. When he ran out of names, Frank led her in silence through the silent city. At last they returned to the first poster, the one which asked for news of Saul, pasted to a post not far from the vacant lot where Frank did his moon watching. Prudence stopped him there; she leaned forward to read the description of the boy and the place where he'd last been seen. —Sad, isn't it? Frank asked.

—Let's go.

—Where?

She read the address from the poster. —It's not far, I think.

Prudence's hand rested on his hip, he knew that, and his hand cupped her shoulder. He remarked how narrow her back was, and how her hair tickled his forearm each time she turned her head. But the buildings around him seemed foggy and insubstantial, almost as though, if Frank squinted, he might be able to see what lay inside them. Prudence stopped in a street where two-story stucco houses slumbered, dark except for the clouds which had settled on the canted roofs and a distant streetlight, which threw the shadow of a bicycle across the pavement. There was no one to be seen but themselves. All the same, Prudence unslung her camera, opened the case, adjusted the aperture and the exposure time. She took one picture, or several, of the spot where Saul had last been seen. Frank wondered what crime the negatives would reveal, if they revealed a crime at all. His side was still warm where Prudence's arm had rested, where her ribs had touched his.

Frank was about to ask her some inane question about the night's victims when, placing one palm on the back of his neck, she kissed his mouth. Her lips were cold. For a long time they stood, wrapped in Frank's coat, at the start of the sleeping street; then the photographer began to shiver and demanded, her teeth chattering, that Frank lead her home. As they walked past the tower of the Painting School and the observatory's dome, Frank wondered whether this was how James had felt when he fell in love with Rosalyn. Though they had not discussed leaving the city recently, Frank thought that it was only a matter of time before he found himself in the photographer's car, driving north into a landscape composed indistinctly of mist, thickets, and slow-croaking frogs.

When he called Prudence the next night there was no answer. Frank went upstairs to his room and looked out the window. The night was clear and bright; her light was on; he could see the vase and the table. He walked around the block to her house, found her name on the bell, and rang. When she didn't answer he climbed the stairs to her room. The door was open; the light marked out a rectangle on the landing. Frank went inside. The room was empty except for the table and the vase. The walls were thin and insubstantial, the floor old and scuffed; the closet contained only a wooden pole, some coat hooks, and a few hangers. Frank looked out the window, wondering what Prudence saw when he was looking at her. But his window was closed, and he had left his lights off; the glass and the dark room had become a mirror for the moon.

FRANK WAITED UNTIL MORNING FOR PRU-
dence to return, but she didn't. He went
back to Mrs. Bellaway's and bleached the
robes by accident, so that pink spots appeared in their fabric, which had to be
dyed black again and then rewashed. It
was late in the evening before he was finished. Mrs. Bellaway was furious, both at
the wasted materials and that he had chosen this moment, when things were particularly tight, to waste them. Frank
called Prudence in the morning. She
didn't answer, and her light was off.
When he returned to her building in the
evening, her name was gone from the list
of names by the row of bells in the
vestibule; he went up anyway, but her
door was locked and no sound came
through it. Frank called the police department from the phone on the corner.

—I'm looking for one of your photographers, he said.

—Got a stiff?

—A what?

—A stiff.

—No, I'm just, I'm looking for a photographer in particular. Her name is Prudence. She works for the police department.

—I'll put you through to Forensics.

—Hello? Frank said when the phone was answered again. I'm looking for a photographer named Prudence.

—She's not here, the person on the other end of the line said.

—Well, when was she there last?

—She's never been here. The person laughed. No one comes here twice.

—That's not what I mean, I mean, isn't there a photographer named Prudence working for you?

—It's Analysis you want, the person said.

—Looking for Prudence, are you?

—Yes.

—Why?

—She's missing. I mean, she hasn't been home in days, and well, we're friends and so I wanted to know . . .

—I'll put you through to Disappearances, then.

—Hello? The person in charge of Disappearances was either laryngitic or very old.

—Hi, yes, I'm looking for—

—Have you submitted a report?

—A what?

—A Disappearance Report. You need to submit a report before we can do anything.

—Yes, well, the person I'm looking for has been gone for a couple of days, so maybe someone else has submitted a report.

—Yes, that's possible. But in that case we can't release the information to you.

—Why not? Isn't it enough that you know she's gone? Isn't it enough that I want to know where she is?

—That depends what you mean by "gone," the quiet voice in charge of Disappearances said. Is she gone in general, or is she gone only from you?

—Gone in general.

—How do you know?

—I went to her room and she wasn't there.

—Yes, well, she might have moved, then, hm?

—She didn't tell me she was moving.

—Exactly. So you'll have to submit a report.

—To who?

—Any police station will take it.

—And then I can call you again?

—We'll contact you as soon as we know something. Goodbye.

The Disappearances clerk hung up.

The police station was the largest building on the block next to Frank's. The hall resembled the waiting room of a train station; windows or booths ran the length of one wall, and long lines stretched before each window. There was nothing else, no desks, no criminals—or at least none in handcuffs—no uniformed officers except the two who flanked the door and stared intently at everyone who entered but said nothing and stopped no one. The line at the DISAPPEARANCES window was the longest of all: it stretched from one end of the hall to the other. Those at the head of the line were sprawled on blankets or wrapped around pillows; the remains of one or even several meals lay scattered around them, and the best-equipped had hampers which looked as though they might contain several meals more. The window was open, to Frank's surprise, and a clerk waited behind it attentively. Before her stood a woman who looked very tired; she held her head in both hands and spoke slowly to the clerk, a few words at a time, with long intervals of silence. Frank had no patience for the woman. —What's taking her so long, he asked the man behind her in line, who had begun to grow a beard while waiting for the clerk. It suited him poorly. When the bearded man was satisfied that Frank wasn't trying to take his place in line, and had communicated this fact to those behind him, he answered: —Don't be impatient.

—But can't she hurry up?

—She's been there for a day and a half already. She's tired, poor woman.

—A day and a half? You mean, standing there?

—Yes, and she's old, look at those calves, hardly any meat on them, and her knees are shaking. She won't hold out much longer.

—But why has she been there so long, if she's so tired?

—She's describing the one she lost.

—That shouldn't take very long. Isn't there a form?

—The form, the bearded man said gravely, is very detailed. It is necessary to tell the office everything you know about the missing person in order to complete it.

—Why everything you know? And why does it take so long to tell?

—How else would the police know who to look for? People resemble one another, by and large. Sometimes the resemblance is very close. The more the police know, the better their chances of laying their hands on the actual missing person, and not a different missing person who only resembles the one you're looking for. In answer to your second question: Can you think of everything at once? Everything you know about a person? These things take time to remember; you have to mull them over, and get at them in different ways, so that no detail escapes you. Fortunately, the police are generous. They give us all the time we want to remember, and don't consider the description finished until we ourselves decide to stop. Only then do they review the information they've been given, and decide whether or not the form is complete.

—So people stand there for days, trying to remember?

—If they're old or infirm or forgetful, yes, usually they stay for a day or two. If they're younger or more deeply attached to the missing one, it can take weeks. Even then—the bearded man sighed—the information usually isn't enough.

—You mean, they don't complete the forms?

—That's right.

—What happens then?

—Nothing. The form is marked incomplete and set aside, and if the one looking remembers something else, they're welcome to get back on line and add it to the report. The police are very generous.

—But why do you wait, if you know that the information isn't going to be complete?

—My information is complete.

—Who are you looking for?

—My wife. No one knew her better than I. We were married thirty years.

—You were? Frank asked, for the bearded man didn't look that old.

—Thirty full years, the happiest of my life. I remember every day of them, almost eleven thousand days, and I can tell you something about each one. Each day was different. I have them all—he tapped the side of his head—here. What could be more complete than that?

—What was she like before you met each other?

—She was nothing before she met me. She told me so herself. It doesn't matter, anyway, the woman I'm looking for is the one I was married to. The bearded man was indignant, and Frank wandered past the other windows, where LICENSES, PERMITS, PAYMENTS, and ACCUSATIONS were issued, accepted, and recorded, and out of the police station altogether.

It was at this point, or really a few days later, that James reentered Frank's life, in the form of a postcard from a city a few days away by rail. Mrs. Bellaway gave the card to Frank with an injunction to be careful with his money. *Dear Frank*, it read, *We're out of money and were wondering if you could loan us some while we look for work. Hope you're well.* Then there was an address, and at the very bottom a note from Rosalyn, which informed Frank that Charles had forgiven all, and would Frank please pay her father a visit? Because he must be lonely in his retirement.

Frank put on his coat at once, and found a bus that crossed the river and dropped him between a muddy tributary and a narrow park teeming with children and dogs. Charles reclined in a hammock stretched between the two trees on his property. His leg had never really mended; broken bones had given way to weakness, and weakness to a tingling that was worse than no sensation at all, as if, Charles said, it was restless but didn't want to go nowhere that I could take it. Carolyn paced from one tree to the other, smoking, turning her head infrequently to make some remark to her father. She had married a plumber. Carolyn complained, —Isn't it awful he's never home and when he's home it's nothing but water, water, water, that's all we talk about. When Frank asked after Evelyn, he was informed that she had run away.

—To where?

Charles shrugged, and Carolyn sighed. —Who knows? She was always an independent girl.

—Have you filed a report?

—Oh, no, they said in unison, she's not missing.

—Well, you don't know where she is, do you?

—Yes, Charles said, I mean no, but missing is different.

They talked until dusk. Charles complained of dreams in which his bad leg led him into all sorts of trouble, kicking and stamping about in a sailor's dance. Aside from that and a tendency to hear watch bells when the wind set to rattling the trees, he admitted that retirement agreed with him. —It gives me time to think, you know, and to make planes. As a hobby, you understand. I make 'em out of wood. For the grandchildren. He nodded at Carolyn, who scowled back. —To keep my hands busy, at any rate, he said. Charles invited Frank to stay for dinner. Frank declined, and walked slowly toward the bus stop, amazed that Charles, his leg, his daughter and yard had appeared in his life again. It gave him hope that other things seen and lost might be recovered.

.   .   .

Frank wandered about, hoping to chance upon familiar faces. He walked with the thought that Prudence might step out of a street door as he passed, or wave at him from the window of the wigmaker's shop that had opened up on the street next to Bell-away's. He fancied that he saw her profile in the windows of the carriages that sometimes rolled out of courtyards for a warm night's drive in the park. Sometimes he saw her alone, and sometimes in the company of the lunar children, at the ends of streets that curved like lenses out of sight; under bridges he saw their moon-whitened arms and legs rolling about, but found when he had climbed down to the foot of the embankment nothing more than a roll of paper, a length of twine, the frame of an umbrella, or a steel ball clattering to a stop on the cobblestones.

Nights, he wandered farther and farther afield, taking the bus when he could and walking when he had to. He looked in vain for the corner where Prudence had taken her last photograph, to see if he could find in it some clue as to where the photographer had gone. In the course of looking, he discovered that there were no less than six rail lines leading out of the city, and that there had once been refineries by the riverbank. He found a network of green canals which ran in rectilinear paths, a sunken garden filled with underwater plants, the paper mill and the tanneries, and a thousand other things which might not have existed at all if he hadn't seen them. His wandering made good no visible loss, but at the end of a month Frank regained the wonder that had carried him through the city when he first arrived: a patient curiosity that wanted nothing to be revealed too quickly. He missed Prudence all the same. On Sunday afternoons Frank brooded, wondering if there might not be some way to draw the total lack of Prudence in his room, her not sitting in the chair and not leaning forward to pick something off the table, turn it over, and put it down again. But it was impossible, even more impossible than drawing death, and even at death he was out of practice.

Having sent no money, he forgot altogether about the postcard from James, until one day James and Rosalyn appeared at the door to Mrs. Bellaway's.

—Hey, James said, it's been an age.

—Yes it has.

James's clothes told the story of his life since he had eloped: he wore a tired pair of respectable shoes, what had once been a respectable shirt, and around his neck a gold medallion of the kind thought to ward off speechlessness, insects, and despair. Rosalyn had simply faded. She clasped her hands and smiled politely at Frank.

—I got your card, Frank said. I'm sorry I couldn't send anything.

—Not to worry. Actually, we have another favor to ask.

—What is it? Of course I'll do it if I can.

—We need to stay with you, just for a few days.

—But, Frank said to Rosalyn, your father?

—He won't let us stay together until we're married. We're waiting for the license now, or really we're about to apply for the license, but it's just a formality. We need to stay with you until we get the license.

—There isn't room.

—Come on, Frank, we don't take up much space. And it's you or the street.

—Mrs. Bellaway won't like it.

—I'll explain it to her, I'll explain everything so that she likes it.

—All right. Frank allowed them in. You'll have to sleep on the floor.

—We're used to that, they said to each other, aren't we?

They stayed for a week, and then another, and soon it became clear that either they had never applied for the license or they had applied but their application would never be processed, or it would be processed, had been processed and turned down on account of some technicality. James played the guitar all day, and Rosalyn, as far as Frank knew, just sat at the table and looked at her hands. At night the three of them went walking. Once Frank took them to the lot where he used to watch the moon, but Rosalyn complained that the bugs were simply eating her alive. On the way home, Frank told them about Prudence, about her disappearance and the steps he had taken to find her.

—Why don't you put up a poster? James said. For the first time Frank felt some goodwill toward his guests. He stayed up all night going through the sketches he had made of Prudence, trying to decide which was the best likeness. It was hard to tell. They were all like her, but each one was like her in a different way, at a different time. In the end he had each drawing made into a poster of its own; he paid for them with the money he had saved from his salary. When the posters were ready he and James covered the city with hundreds of Prudence's faces and, under them, the address where Frank could be found. It took them a long time to find a spot for each poster. They had to tear some of the older ones down, signs made by the parents of children who had been gone for so long that they weren't children anymore, squares of paper warped by the rain and bleached to the color of the sky.

Visitors arrived at Mrs. Bellaway's, asking for Frank. The first to come was a haggard, hook-nosed man with a headband and a beard the color of his stained teeth, who tapped Frank on the arm as he spoke.

—I saw your poster, he said.

—Then you've seen her? Where is she?

—Who?

—Prudence. The girl on the poster.

—Haven't seen her.

—Then why are you here?

—I put up a poster myself, once. Before your time.

—Why did you come here?

—My cousin it was. Took him out for a walk one day, and I let go his wrist, then next thing couldn't find him nowhere, and never did.

—Why are you telling me this?

—I know how you must feel. It's hard at first, but you'll get used to it.

—Get used to what?

—The missing.

—I don't want to get used to the missing, I want to find Prudence, and if you haven't seen her, then I don't think we have anything to talk about.

—Suit yourself. The old man hurried off.

The next day it was a woman a few years older than Frank, who had lost her daughter. Their conversation was more or less the same. Two days after that, a pair of twins showed up and told Frank about the time long ago when they had been triplets. Frank began to wonder whether he should take the posters down, but he couldn't remember where he'd put them all; in any case, he still hoped that they would help him find Prudence. Two or three times a week, someone came by to tell Frank about their own loss. After a while, when the seasonal storms had washed many of the posters away, the visits were less frequent. James and Rosalyn stayed on, playing the guitar and sitting, respectively. They ate their meals out, and, when they made love, did so quietly, in the hours when they hoped that Frank was asleep.

Bonnie appeared on a Sunday afternoon, smiling; when she spoke to Frank she touched him on the hand. She was neatly though eccentrically dressed in a tweed jacket, a tweed skirt, and a hat made from a coil of brassy wire; Frank thought she might be a retired professor or an heiress, escaped from one of the great horse-raising families in the south.

—Are you taking it well? she asked him.

—The disappearance, you mean? It's been a long time now.

—How long?

—Three months.

—Dear boy, that's no time at all. You're young, I know, but you have to let yourself feel these things.

—It's mostly just that I'm tired of people asking about it.

—Then why did you put up the poster?

—What? Because I wanted, because I want to find her.

Bonnie smiled. —That's why I put mine up, of course. But it was a long time ago.

Frank waited for the rest of the story, and it came: the older sister, a somnambulist since she learned to walk, who had been found at daybreak in more and more remote parts of the city, until one night she went to bed and never returned.

—I don't understand, he said.

—Somnambulism? It's like walking in your sleep, but more so.

—No no. I don't understand why you people come here. You haven't seen Prudence, have you?

—Who? Oh, the girl. No.

—Then why?

—We come here to make you a part of the community.

—What community?

—The community of those who remain.

—That's ridiculous.

—The community of those who are looking.

—They don't constitute a community. Each of us has lost someone different. Each missing person has gone to a different place. If we can help each other at all, it's by looking out for the people who are missing, and telling each other when we see them.

—Oh dear, Bonnie said. You'd better come with me.

—Come where?

—Just come. She touched his hand and led him downstairs. They took one bus, and then another, across the river and through the part of the city where the buildings were made of white stone, to the part where they were made of brick, then

black stone, then glass, and then wood and tar paper; in the last
street, where the bus left them, the buildings were made of silver
wood and shingles and long ropes. Frank had forgotten that the
city was on the coast, but he could smell the ocean in the wind,
and ahead of him was a dune; he heard the sound of waves. Bonnie led him up a sagging staircase, over the dune. For the first time
Frank saw the beach, and wondered whether he was seeing it correctly. There was hardly a square foot of sand visible on all its
length, so great was the crowd gathered there. There must have
been hundreds of thousands of people, all of them standing—
there wasn't room to lie down, or even to sit—shoulder to shoulder, and walking back and forth, up and down the coast. Frank
could see only the first rank, the ones closest to the dune; beyond
that there were only shoulders and heads and head-colored dots
and then the ocean. The sound he had thought to be waves turned
out to be feet crunching the sand, and voices murmuring to one
another, all of them crunching and murmuring at once.

—I don't understand, Frank said.

—We've all lost someone, said Bonnie.

—But why come here?

—There's a story, Bonnie said, that this is where they go. The
missing, wherever they disappear from, end up on an island
which you can see just offshore when the tide's out. That's why
some people come here; they push their way as close as they can
to the water, and wait. There's another story, of course, which
says that the missing all end up on the beach, and wander there,
confused. That's why the rest of us come: we walk up and down
through the crowd, looking. Then there's another story: that if

everyone in the city stands on the beach at the same time, the city itself will disappear. That's an old story, and there aren't but a few old people who believe it now.

—Has anyone . . . found anyone?

—Oh! Constantly. We find each other.

—But not the ones you're looking for.

They walked for a moment without speaking.

—Come on, Bonnie said, I'll introduce you. She dragged him into the crowd. She presented Frank again and again to particular friends, who smiled amiably and without curiosity.

—What do you do? they asked.

—Oh, I draw.

—Didn't you see his posters? Bonnie nudged them. Beautiful drawings.

—For a living? they asked.

—Well! as a hobby.

Frank met carpenters and caulkers, sealers and welders and scrubbers and scrapers, painters, drapers, joiners and roofers, bricklayers, window washers, ironmongers, street sweepers, forensic meteorologists, lightning-rod installers and salesmen on credit, buglers, bootblacks, botanists, representatives of all the trades by which the city lived. He even thought he saw Mrs. Bellaway, once, ducking furtively past a rotund mason in order to avoid meeting Frank. When it became dark, the crowd began to disperse, although there were still a fair number of them on the beach when Frank and Bonnie left. Frank looked back at them from the top of the dune: they wandered or didn't wander according to their belief, but talked amiably, lit cigarettes and built fires; they produced kettles and sandwiches and pots of soup and told each other stories to pass the time while they waited for low tide or coincidence. On the bus back to the city it was the same: full of beachcombers, chatting or looking mildly at their reflections in the windows, making engagements to meet again next week and shaking hands before they stepped down from the bus and returned to their houses, whose construction Frank couldn't identify by night.

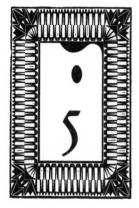

IT WAS UNDERSTOOD THAT FRANK DIDN'T have to see her again if he didn't want to. Bonnie had left that up to him; she patted him on the cheek and told him that she held a salon at her house on Wednesday nights. She wrote her address on a scrap of paper, and explained that there was a bus which mostly ran on time. After two days of thinking and listening to James play the guitar in his room at night, and watching Rosalyn watch her hands as though she were about to learn something from the way they didn't shake, Frank decided to go and see what kind of a salon could be held by a woman in a wire hat.

The bus took him a very long way from his house, to the hills at the edge of the pine forest. Here the houses were taller, and painted white or dove-gray; their windows were shuttered, and the top half of the basement of each house was above-ground, so that the front door could be reached only by climbing a short flight of stairs. The bus, despite Bonnie's assurances, was late. He hurried up the steps and clapped the knocker against the heavy wood of the door. After a minute it was opened by a woman much younger than Bonnie, narrow-framed, whose face would have been pretty if only she paid it a little less attention: it twitched now and then as she corrected the line of her lips and rolled her eyes to check the set of her lashes and brows. A tubular red garment ran from her shoulders to her knees; below that she perched on a pair of very tall, very narrow blue shoes.

—Oh, she said.

Frank held up the piece of paper on which Bonnie had written her address. —Is this where she lives? My name is Frank.

—Yes, Frank. The woman smiled. I'm Ernest. Please come in.

—Ernest?

—I'm Bonnie's daughter. Ernest looked back as she led him down a long hallway, its pale wood floor covered by pink and green braided rugs.

—Very nice to meet you, Frank said.

Ernest brought him into the main room of the house: a bright hall two stories high with a fire going in a hearth at one end and large red cushions along the walls, where the guests were invited to sit. Most of them were already sitting when Frank arrived. They had folded their legs up and rested their chins on their fists and closed their eyes attentively, listening to a tall woman who stood with her back to the hearth and spoke from a sheaf of notes. She stopped when Ernest came in and smiled at the two of them. Frank smiled back, hesitantly, and found that the guests were looking at him with more interest than he could justify, knowing what he did about himself. Bonnie, who had been sitting nearest to the speaker, rose and made the introductions:

—This is Frank, my discovery. He draws. And this—she waved—is the salon. Find a cushion and listen.

Frank sat between Ernest and a serious young man with nervous hands and skin the color of fluorescent light. The speaker resumed. It took Frank a good deal of listening to narrow down the possible topics of her story to two or three, so strange were her words and so winding her diction, as though she were not reading from her notes but translating, as though the papers which she shuffled quickly as she talked were in fact the fragments of an ancient philosophical work which she was reconstituting on the spot for the benefit of the salon. It was either an epic poem, of the kind which Frank's school had assured him it was important to read—only somewhat later on in a different school—or it was a manual for doing something complicated with tools the likes of which Frank had never seen, or it was a history in verse of the construction of something. After a few minutes, when the young man had stopped pulling on his fingers and Ernest had relaxed into her cushion in such a way that her tubular something fell away from her knees, Frank understood that it was the history of the early days of the city. The tall woman was speaking of the time when there had been no city at the junction of the river and the sea, only a vast expanse of dunes held in place by marsh grasses and the stony nests of enormous birds. It was the birds, she said, who had plucked the first man and the first woman out of the sea, where they had drifted in the wake of a shipwreck of which they were the only survivors. The birds had carried the man and the woman in their claws out of the water and deposited them in their nest, where the nestlings found them thoroughly unpalatable. So the man and the woman, more

alarmed in some ways by their rescue than by the prospect of drowning, crawled out of the nest and built themselves a shack of driftwood. They started a fire, the first fire, and fed themselves eagerly on seared kelp and the unhatched eggs of the giant birds. Soon the man and the woman made children and houses; they stripped the kelp from the dunes, and drove the birds farther and farther afield, until there was nothing left to hold the dunes together, and the time of the great sandstorms began. Their children combined fire and sand to make glass, and dirt and water baked into brick; then the glassblowers and bricklayers learned how to fish, there being few other sources of food left at the mouth of the river. So the city, by the time it became a city, was full of fishermen and fishmongers and fishwives; the first markets sold fish, dried, smoked, and glazed, and bricks made more sturdy by the addition of fish bones; they sold fishing poles of driftwood, hooks of glass, and creels of reed and mud. All the other crafts came about as a result of these first few arts: the building of houses out of wood, mud, and glass, the entrapment of birds and other animals. The first story told in the city was the *Fish Edda*, which held that the first man and woman were delivered from the mouth of a giant fish; it was only later that mythographers, ornithologists, and ichthyologists uncovered the story of the shipwreck and the giant birds. And this, the speaker concluded, is how the city began.

The guests rubbed their heads and stomachs reflectively, or murmured to their neighbors. Ernest settled into a position in which less of her legs could be seen. A heavyset man with brilliant white hair and a thin smile spoke first:

—I'm sure you meant to explain it, he said, but how are they supposed to have started the fire?

—Fire was innate within the wood.

The heavyset man was satisfied with this, and noted it in a book which he then replaced in his pocket.

A dour woman in a cowl asked, —What would have happened if the woman had not got along with the man?

—Or vice versa, said the young man who sat next to Ernest.

—Love means nothing when you live in a bird's nest.

From the salon's approving murmurs Frank understood that the question had been difficult, and that the tall woman had answered it adroitly.

—Can we know the date of the shipwreck? asked a man in a cleric's tight collar.

—The fish skeletons and the bird skeletons have been counted. But we can only know the date approximately.

The cleric sat down, and no one rose to take his place. It seemed to Frank that the assembled members of the salon were waiting for him to speak. As he'd come late, he didn't know what to ask, but in order not to disappoint Bonnie he stood up and cleared his throat.

—What I'd like to know is, if the man and the woman were the first man and woman, then where did the ship come from?

It was as though he'd asked her to define the sun, or to tell him why water ran downhill. Each member of the salon, at the same time, found something engrossing to watch in a different part of the room. The speaker shuffled her note cards; the heavyset man glared at Frank from under lowered brows. Ernest giggled and covered her mouth with her hand.

—Well, I think we're finished for tonight, Bonnie announced. Why don't you all help yourselves to a drink?

They filed into the dining room, where bottles crowded a table. Frank was the last to rise. He wanted to go straight out of the house, to the bus stop, and never to return, but Bonnie took his arm. —That was a good question, you know, she said gently. It's just that they've been talking about the same thing for so long they practically have their own language, if you know what I mean.

—What are they talking about?

—Why, justice, of course, Bonnie said.

Then, as Frank looked bewildered, she pushed him toward the other room. —And don't pay any attention to what they tell you. They aren't used to you yet, that's all. Just enjoy yourself, Bonnie said, and guided him into the crowd.

Justice, Frank thought, on the bus home. Well, who didn't want that? Only it wasn't clear what sort of justice they meant, or what it had to do with bricks and fish and giant birds. The bus lurched around a corner; a sign in the shape of an enormous pink head leered in through the window, then hurried away, an advertisement for something. Frank wondered where Prudence was now. Had she left the city? Or was she still here, was she trapped, waiting for someone—for Frank—to free her? He imagined her face broken into slivers by bars, her pale form seen through the window of a high tower. If only he stood at the foot of the tower, he would find a way to climb up, and let himself in, and then, and then.

When Frank reached Bellaway's, James and Rosalyn were asleep. The night lights in the windows opposite had gone out, and in every window but one the morning lights were coming on.

·   ·   ·

The city went on vacation; the streets emptied and virtually everything closed down. Frank went back to the salon when the season had turned and people were wearing jackets again. He arrived early this time, and found a seat opposite Ernest, who was wedged between Max, the nervous young man, and the cowled woman, whose name was Margarete. The speaker that night was the heavyset man with silver hair, Lastrade of the Quadrilateral University, emeritus. He took a long time to compose himself before the hearth, folded his hands behind his back, brought them out again, looked them over, then put them away, took a deep breath, and began. The story he told was about a time when the city had been ruled by a monarch, who raised a palace on the spit of land which stuck out from the mouth of the river into the sea. He named the palace Justice and surrounded it with a high wall. This particular king, who was neither the first of his dynasty nor the last, but in fact was a rather undistinguished king in other respects, had a great fondness for the sound of his own words. Not so much for the sound of them, actually, Lastrade elaborated with glee, as for the echo of their sound: he liked to hear his words proclaimed loudly into open spaces, so that reverberations would reach him where he sat in the center of his palace, and he would no longer have any idea what he had said, but would recognize it as his own. The king wrote a great number of edicts without much regard to their content, and had them all read aloud so that they became law. Finally, in order to hear the syllables of his laws as clearly as possible, he surrounded the palace wall with a great empty space, and at the edge of it he raised an even higher wall, and wrote an edict which made it punishable by death to stand in this empty space when subsequent edicts should be read aloud. This meant, of course, Lastrade explained proudly, that it was impossible to hear the subsequent laws when they were pronounced, and, as they multiplied rather than decreased in number, the mysterious laws became so oppressive that there was soon a revolution; the king was deposed and his palace thrown down. As he went to the scaffold the king said, of course, that the city would from his death on be cursed; he said that, since the rebels had torn his palace down, there would be no more Justice in the city ever again, a proposition which the rebels disagreed with so violently that they beheaded him on the spot. The king's nephew was crowned shortly thereafter, but declined to build a palace; instead, he lived in a pavilion in the middle of the park until he died suddenly of pneumonia; after that, the kings lived like everyone else, in houses and apartments, although somewhat larger, concluded Lastrade, than yours and mine.

—I have a question, the cleric said. What were the laws?

—Yes, said the tall woman, whose name was Chloe, and how many of them were there?

Lastrade was annoyed; he coughed, ran his hand through his white hair, then coughed again. —Only a few fragments of the law books have survived. We have the text of four laws issued by this particular king, whom we assume to be the one responsible for the construction of the palace. There was a law against spitting into the river, and a law against intoxication of all kinds. There was a law against setting fire to dry brushwood in the summer, and a law against saying the name of the king in any enclosed space outside the walls of the palace. He was, you see, afraid of gossip.

—Why did the revolutionaries crown another king, Margarete asked. —Why didn't they overthrow the monarchy altogether?

—It was at a time when other forms of government had not yet been invented, Lastrade announced decisively. Any other questions?

Frank kept quiet.

At a word from Bonnie, the members of the salon rose to drink. Frank stopped Ernest on her way out, and, taking her arm, said, —Can I ask you something?

Ernest laughed sharply. —Why, Frank, she said, when everyone else had left the room, you're very forward.

—You must know what all this is about.

—All what?

—These stories . . .

—Oh. Ernest yawned. They're awfully dull, aren't they? I can hardly stay awake. And that Lastrade! Thinks he's so important. I'll tell you a secret, if you like, Ernest murmured.

—What?

—That's not his hair.

She laughed again, a sound like someone stepping on a creaky floor. —Isn't it awful?

—But, I mean, what are they all doing?

Ernest sighed. —Do you think I'm pretty, Frank?

—Well . . . yes.

—Bonnie says you're a very good artist. Do you have a studio?

—No, just where I live.

—Really? Well. Still, I'd like to come and see your paintings, sometime. Do you ever have . . . you know . . . models?

Ernest smoothed her hair.

—I've been told I'm statuesque, she said.

—I wouldn't know, Frank said. I'm not a sculptor.

—Oh! Ernest scowled at Frank and hurried away.

Frank became a regular, though perplexed, visitor to the salon. Margarete, whose voice was as quiet and as heavy as the fall of a velvet curtain, described how the first crops had been planted in the fields where the factories now stood. She described the discovery of bread and the all-powerful bakers' guild which cut the bread with sawdust in times of shortage, and charged too much in times of plenty, but kept the city's inhabitants enthralled by baking its loaves in a different shape every year, so that there was always something to look forward to. It wasn't clear whether this story was intended to supplant the first story, about the fishermen, or whether it was about a different period in the history of the city; and this question was considered at length in the discussion which followed. The next week Bonnie told a story of no consequence whatsoever, about a young girl who sang in the streets and carried a lantern about for money (it was in the days when the city was lit only intermittently at night); the girl was heard by a famous composer for the opera, who made the songs into arias, and ensured the fame of the city's orchestra and its conservatory. It was, in fact, because of these arias that the money was raised to build what was now the Old Opera House, located in the part of the city where the buildings were made of stone (as opposed to the New Opera House, which was in the part where they were made of glass). When Bonnie's story was over, the audience shifted uncomfortably, as though she had told something about herself which they would have preferred not to know. Next it was Ernest's turn; Frank listened attentively as she told the story of a great popular revolution, brought on by a shortage of bread, and how the houses of the aristocrats, which at that time were made of wood, were torn apart and made into boats, and the aristocrats were forced to row the fishermen far enough offshore that they could catch fish big enough to feed themselves and all their relatives. She spoke deftly and with an air of conviction, but while Frank admired her story, he wondered whether Ernest herself believed it to be true, or whether she had made it up to tie the previous stories together, so that a single history of the city might emerge from the salon, which seemed unlikely to happen otherwise.

The boy, Max, told the story of a judge who had lived in the city long ago. The judge, whose name was Forenses, fell in love with a beautiful woman named Philomena, and married her, but she died of lycanthropy soon afterwards. Forenses, deranged by loss, had the moon arrested for murder—for this was in the days when the heavens did not keep aloof from human affairs, but could be seen now and then in the market, or in the upper balconies of the opera. He summoned all the city's magistrates to try the satellite. Forenses himself wrote the brief for the prosecution, and it was such a marvel of rhetoric that many who heard it went straight home and painted their windows black, that no moonlight might enter their houses again. Moon, perorated Forenses, you have conspired with madmen to deafen the city with howling; you have abetted thieves and cutthroats, and given succor to adulterers and wantons; you have fraudulently changed the line of our coasts, enticing ships to beach and swimmers to drown; you have incited the moths to riot, and the dogs to disturb the peace, astronomers to idleness, and rivers to flood. Countless are the ills which you have brought to the city, and now you add to the catalogue of your crimes a most vile and groundless murder! It is too much; you must hang for it. The magistrates convicted the moon on all counts, and ordered it straightaway to the gallows. Before it was taken from the dock, however, Forenses asked the moon if it had anything to say in its own defense. The moon regarded him coolly; after a moment it spoke: Because you, Forenses, have misjudged me so, it said, I curse you, and all the city's judges, forever to err. Then the moon was hanged, and because of the grave crimes it had been convicted of, no one dared to cut it down; to this day, its body dangles from the scaffold, turning slowly in and out of the light. Forenses's triumph was short-lived: no sooner had the moon been put to death than citizens began to vanish from the city at an alarming rate. It got so bad that justice could no longer be administered; no sooner was a criminal caught than he vanished; or else the arresting officer vanished and the criminal ran away. Forenses ordered an investigation, but half the detectives assigned to the matter disappeared and the other half resigned their commissions in terror. Resolved to find the missing himself, Forenses took a year-long leave from his court, and wandered the city disguised as an ordinary citizen. He learned that, although beloved by his fellow judges, he was tremendously unpopular among the common people, who held him, and not the moon, responsible for the city's ills; but he did not learn where the missing went. After a year, Forenses left the city. He wandered north and south, west and east, and learned much about the country whose laws he knew so well. At last he came to a valley irrigated by green canals which seemed to flow from no source; he hired a boat to scull him upstream and whether he found the missing there or not no one can say, for he never came back down. The rest of the judges, alarmed, set off on a double search, first, to see where the missing had gone, and second, to find Forenses. As the months of their wandering grew to years, the judges forgot their courts and cares. They learned to keep diaries and to paint little watercolors of the landscape, taught themselves to play musical instruments and gave concerts in provincial towns. The provinces were the better for it, and the city none the worse, for its citizens had felt themselves to be beneath trial ever since Forenses pronounced sentence on the moon.

When the questions were over and everyone had taken a drink or two, Frank approached Max. —I enjoyed your story, he said.

—Story?

—Well, it didn't really happen. Did it?

—You're not very quick, are you? See here. We can't just speak of things the way they are, or it would mean jail for all of us.

—Why?

—It's on account of the police, Max said in a low voice. They'd arrest us.

—But, what for?

—Oh, they'd trump up some charge. Meeting at night in a private residence without a permit to assemble, for example.

—No, Frank said, I mean, why would they arrest you in the first place?

—For speaking.

—Is that a crime?

—Who's to say, now that the judges are gone?

—But they're not gone, Frank said. There are lots of judges at Mrs. Bellaway's . . .

—Oh, well, yes. But you can't expect justice from *them.*

—Why not?

—Haven't you seen them?

Frank admitted that he had not. —What do you want, then?

—What we want . . . Max stared past Frank's shoulder at the window with such fixity that Frank was sure someone or something was there. He turned to look, but there was nothing, only the white fluttering of moths around a streetlamp. Max told Frank how the salon aimed at something grand, and noble, like a great building made all of white marble, where cool winds would soothe every affliction, and solid doors keep out all harm. But, he admonished, in order for this building to be put up it would be necessary first to tear down a number of insalubrious structures, tenements of brick and metal, and there were those, did Frank see? who didn't want them torn down. By this point Frank wasn't sure whether he was talking about real buildings, or only about something like buildings, but he nodded because Max expected it. —It's dangerous work, Max said, and we'll all be tried before it's over. You understand?

—Are you . . .

—Ssh! said Max. He wagged a finger. —Just say yes.

—Yes.

—Right. Max took Frank's elbow amicably, and squeezed it between his thumb and forefinger. Frank wondered whether this was some sort of secret gesture, but before he could ask—before he remembered that he didn't have the words to ask—Max was gone, to an alcove where Ernest was waiting, her violet dress trembling like a thrown-back curtain.

Frank waited at the base of the tower. Any day now, he thought, he would be called upon to carry a strangely heavy parcel from the railway station to the museum vestibule, or the telephone would murmur a place and a time where, in darkness, cloaked figures would hand him a rifle and a picture—a sketch, on flimsy paper which would, in a moment, burn of its own accord—of the face he was ordered to destroy. His imagination threw up barricades and overturned buses; shops caught fire and cast lines of smoke into the autumn sky. Then, over the crackle of the fire, a familiar voice would call out, and Frank would charge into the flames with drawn sword (although up until that moment he'd been holding a rifle). In the burnt-out shell of a tower, he'd find Prudence, her face smudged with soot but otherwise unchanged. For some reason, she would be asleep, and it would fall to Frank to kneel beside her, to stroke her shoulder and kiss her cheek. —There's justice, he told himself. To bring her back: that would be justice at last.

The weeks grew heavy with anticipation, then soggy with winter, and nothing changed. One by one the members of the salon rose and told their stories, were questioned, retorted, but nothing was decided, not within their stories, which contradicted one another, and all the less in the world without, where buses rattled on their routes, and smoke rose only from licensed bonfires in the parks and squares. Somewhere in the muddle of stories which were not stories, nor, exactly, anything else, Frank must have lost hold of his memory of Prudence. Or rather, he hadn't lost his memory of her entirely, but only his memory of the whole of her.

He could still see very clearly what her eyes had looked like, and the cast of her chin; he knew the precise degree of warmth he'd felt when she pressed herself to him and told him that, of all the things she loved, she loved silence most of all. Without the real Prudence to bind these thoughts together, however, Frank's memories tended to get confused with other things. He paid undue attention to Chloe's nose and to the warmth of the fireplace; when Margarete spoke he heard Prudence's voice instead.

Prudence and the city dissolved together in Frank's imagination. He tried now and then to draw pictures of the scenes described at the salon, but found that he could not get the proportions right, or that the whole drawing ended up in an odd corner of the page; he tried to draw the salon itself, but found that he remembered the stories better than he did their speakers. James, at least, had found a job preparing solvents for a firm which specialized in cleaning cameras and other delicate apparatuses; he came home late at night, smelling of something like vinegar, and slept soundly until morning, when he went out again. Frank was alone with Rosalyn in the evenings. At first he found this uncomfortable, because she said nothing, and, when he asked her a question, said that she would have to think about it and then never answered. After a while he grew used to having her there; she watched her hands while Frank drew, and didn't look up when he noisily crumpled whatever it was that he had been drawing and threw the ball of paper into the fireplace, where it ignited with a hiss and a puff of smoke.

One Sunday Frank returned to the ocean in the company of Bonnie and Ernest, on whom Bonnie thought he had some design. In truth, he was happy just to set his work aside: the drawings weren't going well; and James was sitting with Rosalyn on the sofa in his room, serenading her in a whisper as he scrubbed his clothes clean of the chemicals which stained them over the course of the week.

They waited for the bus, which was a long time coming, then for the second bus, and once again Frank found himself on the beach without much sense of how he had come to be there. They trudged over the rise of the dune. A sea of hats had replaced the sea of heads; the clomping of feet was heavier and the pace perhaps a bit brisker, but the crowd was as large as it had been the first time. Ernest took Frank's arm; they walked together toward one end of the beach, by the refinery, and then toward the other, where the sand gave way to a strip of marshy land dotted with tidepools, and a stand of pine trees. Ernest began to complain of the cold well before evening, and so they walked back toward the bus stop, arm in arm, as before. Before they reached it, though, an old, inquisitive man with a flat face and wide gray eyes stopped them —Excuse me, he said, and Bonnie introduced them all: Conrad, an industrialist who owned a watch and telescope factory; he was married to an old friend of Bonnie's who volunteered in the textile museum.

—Excuse me, excuse me, he said to Bonnie and Ernest, and to Frank: —Come over here. He tugged at Frank's arm.

When they were ten or fifteen feet from the bulk of the crowd he stopped. —You're the one, aren't you, that's made the drawings?

—You mean, the posters?

—Of the girl, yes, yes. I thought you might be the one, when Bonnie told me about you. Lovely drawings.

—Thank you.

—I was wondering . . . Conrad leaned forward slyly.

—What?

—If you make them on commission.

—The drawings? No, just for pleasure.

—Yes of course, that's what she said—he emphasized the word *said*—but mightn't you accept a commission, if someone offered it?

—I might, Frank supposed.

—That's what I thought. I have a—yes, well, you understand that I won't be able to pay you very much, but I have a request?

—For what?

—It's for my brother.

—He wants a drawing?

—No. Needs a drawing. He's missing, these past ten years.

—Did you file a report?

—Yes, very funny, ha ha. I put up a poster, with a very accurate description.

—And?

—Well, you know how it is. Sympathy, of course, that's very good, and of course that's how I met Bonnie and then my wife. But . . .

—You haven't found him.

—I haven't found him. Conrad nodded as though it were something to be agreed upon, and took Frank's arm again. Will you draw him?

—Your brother? I've never seen him.

—I know that, of course you haven't, but I can describe him to you, so it'll be just like seeing him. It's just that I'm hoping, with a poster . . .

—I haven't had any luck with mine, Frank said.

—Yes well, our cases may be different. For you it's been?

—Nine months. Give or take.

—For me ten years, so perhaps he's due to turn up.

Frank shrugged. —I'll draw him if you like.

—Wonderful! Conrad clapped. I'll pay you what I can. Twenty dollars for the drawing, and another twenty if he's found.

—I'll draw him for free, if you like.

—You mustn't say that. Never do anything for free. You are a professional, you are independent, you must never give yourself away. Sunday, then? Conrad pushed him back in the direction of Bonnie and Ernest. —Around three?

So Frank received his first commission. Drawing from descriptions wasn't as hard as he feared: Conrad came to his room and talked and talked, and in the end threw enough words into the air that, as they settled, the outlines of his brother's face became distinct. Conrad was pleased with the likeness; he gave Frank the twenty dollars quickly and then hurried off, perhaps afraid that, if he let his satisfaction show, Frank would raise his fee on the spot. Frank didn't know what to do with the money as it was; he and James and Rosalyn went out to a restaurant with tall plate-glass windows and a singer and a great bustle of waiters in black; they chattered happily as they ate, and even Rosalyn spoke with great decisiveness, pronouncing judgment on the hands, manicured and otherwise, of all those in the room.

After that, the commissions came quickly. Frank discovered, to his surprise, that almost every member of the salon wanted a portrait drawn or painted, all of absent lovers, friends, and relatives; all of them willing to pay. Lastrade was missing a son, and Margarete her grandparents; Chloe, the woman who had told the first story, was an orphan, as was Max. He made a drawing for each of them, sometimes two or three, in ink or charcoal or watercolor according to the preference of the client, working most of the time from a verbal description of the subject but occasionally from an old photograph. Where he had had no success at all in drawing the murdered, Frank discovered that he had a talent for the faces of those who had disappeared. His clients slipped the drawings gently into specially prepared portfolios; they shook his hand warmly or kissed him on the cheek; Chloe began to cry and threw her arms around his neck, and it was a good quarter of an hour before Frank could break free and prepare his materials for the next customer. The money came in, and Bonnie urged him to quit his job as a washer of robes and take up portraiture full-time. Frank kept the job, though, as much because he couldn't imagine drawing all day as because he feared that the money would dry up as quickly as it had come. He spent it on James, on Rosalyn, on clothes for himself and presents for Ernest; he brought her a different bauble in brass or glass or steel or china every Wednesday night. If Frank was surprised to find himself busy, he was even more so when he saw the posters. Every client who had bought a drawing from him had turned it into a poster, and every poster had been printed and glued to a vertical surface somewhere in the city, so that no matter where he went he saw his own handiwork, some sketches better than others, but all distinctly his. Saul, 13, last seen in a blue-and-yellow shirt and carrying a green bag, was there, and so was Mona the beloved wife; even Mrs. Bellaway's nephews John and Lawrence were to be found somewhere, rendered to the best of Frank's abilities.

Frank had a reputation, at the salon and elsewhere; the men from whom he bought bread and fruit smiled at him knowingly, and Mrs. Bellaway opened the door of the laundry when Frank was working so that her visitors could have a peek at the great artist of the missing.

THE TWO DETECTIVES WERE WAITING FOR Frank in his room when he returned from the salon the next Wednesday night. They were sitting on the sofa, side by side; James and Rosalyn perched in the window nook and watched them with the faces of frightened birds.

—Frank, they're . . . James blurted as Frank opened the door to his room. The detectives stood up, dusting their hands and smiling.

—MacDougall, one of them said. This is my partner, Fallow. MacDougall wore a long russet mustache; his nose lay flat against his upper lip so that he seemed to be viewing the world with his face pressed to an invisible windowpane. Fallow, thinner than his partner, had a jaundiced face and long black hair; he wore a shiny hat and drab coat, and passed his gloves uneasily from one hand to the other without giving any sign that he was aware of doing so. —Sorry to drop in like this, MacDougall apologized. Made your friends nervous. Criminals? Are they?

—No, Frank said. What do you want?

—We hear that you're an artist. MacDougall was the one who spoke; Fallow paced back and forth behind him, now twirling a paintbrush in one hand as though unsure how it worked. —Good business?

—Not really. Sometimes.

—Good money?

—These past few weeks.

—Keep your own hours, do you? Sleep in the day and paint, paint, all night long?

—I work in the laundry, downstairs.

—Yes, hm, of course, of course you do. Ever think about painting on the job? Think about your, ah, next composition?

—No. What's that got to do with anything?

—Just wondering. How long does one of these portraits take you?

—An hour, two hours, it depends.

—Depends, does it? On the medium, I suppose. Watercolors are harder, I suppose, because you have to mix the colors just right. Hm?

—Mostly it depends on the description.

—The description? You mean, the size of the canvas, that sort of thing?

—The description of the person I'm drawing. Some of them are better than others, they're easier to see, and those are the ones that take less time. Frank explained these things slowly, afraid that he wasn't making much sense. He had never met a detective before, but decided instinctively that it would be better if he was polite.

—Description of the person, hm, hm. MacDougall turned

around. You get that, Fallow? Fallow put down the brush and shook his head.

—I don't get it. You say you have a description of the person you're drawing?

—Yes.

—They aren't here?

—No.

—You don't draw them, what is it, from life?

—No, of course not.

—Of course not?

—Of course not, because they're missing, that's why people pay me to draw them.

MacDougall licked his lips.

—You draw them, hmm, because they're missing. It seemed a revelation to him. Even Fallow stopped, lifted his hat, and scratched beneath it, whether out of surprise or for other reasons Frank couldn't tell. He looked at James and Rosalyn, who were both white as judges' linen. James shook his head slowly.

—Let me understand you. People pay you to draw other people, who aren't here? And this is your business? MacDougall asked slowly.

—That's right.

—Good! Then we've got the right man. Before Frank could blink, MacDougall had seized his wrist, twisted it behind his back, and placed it firmly within a metal cuff, which pinched; soon the other wrist was similarly bound. —You'll come with us.

—But it's not illegal, is it? Frank asked.

—If it were up to *me*, MacDougall said, I'd let you do it all day, and all night, too, if you wanted. I might even come in and ask you to draw one or two people with quite amusing faces, just to see if you're as good as you're said to be. I'd have the drawings framed. He yanked on the cuffs, and Frank had no choice but to follow him to the door. —Have them framed and hang them in my parlor. I have a little spot above the sideboard where they'd go quite well, don't you think, Fallow?

Fallow shrugged.

—I think they'd go quite well there. MacDougall pushed Frank into the hall.

Frank considered running away, down the stairs, but with his hands bound he was almost sure to trip and fall on the winding flights which led to the street; as for asking Mrs. Bellaway to help him, she was usually asleep at this hour, and was famous for her ill temper when suddenly awakened.

—But, MacDougall said, it's not up to me, and so we're taking you to the chief of police. Well, goodbye, little criminals, he said to James and Rosalyn. With Fallow leading the way and Mac-Dougall behind, they went downstairs, where a police car was waiting. Fallow opened the door, and MacDougall pushed Frank into the back seat, separated from the front by a grille.

They drove a long way, and crossed the river twice. Frank couldn't remember whether the river itself curved, and so couldn't tell whether the police were simply trying to confuse him. As they drove, MacDougall quizzed him on the technical aspects of his work as a portraitist. —How do you shade, he asked, and how do you arrange your drawing so that, when it's done, it's centered on the page? How much water do you need to produce a good, accurate sky-blue? And what's the best way to paint a perfect gray? A pitch-black? Frank didn't know whether he was

expected to give a confession or a lesson in art. They drove through the old part of the city, where the streets more often than not ended in squares without issue. Fallow stopped the car outside a brown, almost featureless building, screened by old trees and encircled by an iron fence in which ornate capitals were wrought: a former aristocratic compound. A crowd waited outside the gate, waving cameras and notebooks.

—Is this the artist? one of the reporters yelled, as Fallow dragged Frank from the car.

—Did he resist arrest?

—Does he live in squalor?

—Who were his associates?

—Have we seen the end of it? Or can we expect imitators?

—Artist! Have you got anything to say to the press?

MacDougall pushed Frank past them before he could answer, and, in truth, Frank wasn't sure what he would have said. Just when they were clear of the crowd, the detectives turned and posed, with Frank between them, long enough for a dozen flashbulbs to pop and hiss, and a dozen shutters to click with a sound like the chattering of teeth. It was, Frank realized, the first time his picture had ever been taken. Then the detectives did a brisk about-face and, with the criminal in tow, disappeared into the headquarters of the chief of police.

The building consisted chiefly of corridors, offices, and staircases leading up to other corridors and offices. MacDougall and Fallow, scorning the narrow stairs which they were accustomed to climb for everyday use, led Frank up the great marble staircase at the center of the building, a relic of the days when one of the city's governing families lived there. It was reserved now for ceremonial purposes. The chief's office was on the seventh and topmost floor. On the third floor a grizzled sergeant took one of MacDougall's hands in both his own. His eyes were wet. —God bless you for getting the bastard, he said, pointing at Frank; I've got two little ones of my own. On the fourth floor, a detective kissed Mac-Dougall on both cheeks and whispered into his ear; on the fifth, a captain of police took Fallow aside, and, with his arm around the detective's shoulders, began —I've had my eye on you for a long time, boy. On the sixth floor, Frank was ordered to wait outside the frosted door of an inspector's office, while, within, two silhouettes clinked glasses and threw their heads back, laughing. A minute later MacDougall stepped out again, a brighter shade of red than before, mumbling to himself, —By God, today of all days . . . By the time they had reached the seventh floor, MacDougall and Fallow walked arm in arm, leaving Frank to follow in their entourage, which had grown as they climbed. Detectives and lieutenants, inspectors and captains and even an adjunct commissioner followed them along the corridor, calling out congratulations. MacDougall began to sing, and Fallow joined in, as did the rest:

O Liza my darling the life of an officer
Is nothing but work and dismay.
O, I'd much rather be a poor clerk whining "Coffee, sir?"
Or a lawyer declaiming in re;
Or a bailiff who leads the accused to the dock
Or a judge with ferocious expressions
Or a jailer who jangles his key in the lock
Or a priest hearing final confessions.
The hangman who tightens the noose so the women'll

Cheer has it better than I.
But I thank my sweet stars I was not born a criminal
So Liza O Liza don't cry
So Liza O Liza don't cry...
O Liza my darling don't cry!

The police applauded and tumbled, still laughing, into the chief's office. Frank was by this time at the back of the crowd; he could see almost nothing of the office: only that it was low and larger than the rest. Afraid, suddenly, that he might be overlooked, and so vanish forever into the atrociously cheerful bustle of the police station, Frank pushed his way forward, elbowing even the adjunct commissioner aside, until he reached the chief's desk. One of the detectives had pushed Frank's cap down over his eyes out of spite, so that all he could see were the dark, burled wood of the desk and the hands of the chief of police. They were extraordinarily white hands, with long fingers, the hands of a pianist or a model for fashionable gloves. They cradled a crystal inkwell and a little harness bell, a souvenir perhaps, which jingled in the chief's hand.

—Aha! MacDougall said, catching sight of Frank. The prisoner!

—This is the artist? the chief asked. His voice was high and piercing. Frank wondered if the chief were very old—it was not impossible to imagine an old man belonging to such white hands—or if he were perhaps very young, or dwarfish, and trying to dissimulate the size of his body by extending his voice beyond its capacity.

—This is the one, MacDougall said.

—Who made the posters?

—The very one.

—The missing-person posters? The chief uttered these words with great contempt.

—We've brought him to you, MacDougall announced, just as you asked.

—Young man, the chief addressed Frank sternly, I have only one question for you. What did you hope to accomplish by these acts?

—Why, nothing, Frank said.

—You see! He's an anarchist! said MacDougall.

—Are you aware of the consequences of your rash actions? the chief continued.

—Consequences?

—A nihilist! said MacDougall.

—Who put you up to this?

—No one, really. I did it myself.

—A solipsist! And a liar! MacDougall crowed.

—Do you realize that, because of you, thousands of innocent people will suffer?

—But I didn't—

—Mass suicides would not be surprising, the chief interrupted. They usually accompany great social unrest. We can expect riots, too, and arsonists, and malingerers. The police are going to have a job of it, after what you've done. Why, it won't surprise us in the least if there are hijackers and highwaymen, purse-snatchers and kidnappers and home-wreckers, vitriol- throwers and con artists, panderers and procurers and touts, criminals and vermin and lowlife of all descriptions on the prowl, right now, because of your posters. The hospitals will be overcrowded, of course, and the sick will be turned away at doctors' doors, and pregnant women will die for lack of proper midwifery; children will grow up uneducated and adults will grow slack and lazy. Then there are the street cleaners to think of: they're going to have to work around the clock sweeping up anarchists' tracts; the police will overextend themselves trying to protect the street cleaners, and the shopkeepers will close up shop for lack of police protection, and the distributors will close down for lack of shops, and the factories will stop producing, and profits will decline, and stockholders will complain, and the milk of nursing mothers will sour, and half the city will be awake in the middle of the night, taking advantage of the other half. It's a terrible thing you've done, boy.

—But what have I done? Drawn a few pictures?

—Pictures! The chief made a spitting sound. And of whom!

—Of missing persons.

—Of missing persons! Do you know what you're saying? Do you know what's happening, now that your pictures are plastered like plague-spots on every wall of this great city? The citizens are losing faith in their police! When that's gone, there will be nothing left. Only anarchy, and nihilism, and a Dark Age to rival all the ones we've already had! Is that what you want?

—No . . .

—Did you stop to think, when you drew these, these pictures, that the police might already be working on the problem? Did you stop to think that there were already channels through which the missing could be located? That people were paying you to willfully and deliberately circumvent the procedures established for their own good? Did you? Did you?

—No.

—Did you think that people might lose their faith in science and police procedure, and renounce all their good common sense in favor of your superstitious quackery? Fetishes! That's what they are, your posters! Heathen idols, voodoo dolls, nostrums and placebos! You have undermined the city's health! What do you think will happen if the responsibility for the recovery of the missing is taken from the capable hands of the police and divvied up like a loaf of dry bread among the masses?

—Perhaps, Frank said dryly, some of the missing will be found.

—It's no use! the chief roared. He's deaf! He won't hear us! A hardened nut! Lock him up.

—Wait! Frank called back. Don't I have the right to a trial?

—A trial? The chief sounded genuinely astonished. What for? Have you committed a crime?

—Yes! I mean, no! I'm innocent!

—Then there's no need for a trial, surely. The officers laughed, and the chief laughed with them, his good cheer restored. MacDougall and Fallow adjusted Frank's hat and led him downstairs to a service entrance at the rear of the building, which let onto an alley pocked with pools of dark water. In no time at all, Frank was back in the police car; Fallow turned on the siren and they careened off, wailing.

The prison was at the eastern edge of the city, by the ocean. It appeared first as a glow on the horizon, then as a white spot at the end of streets, visible when they passed a vacant lot or turned onto a wide avenue; then it was a growing collection of white shapes at the end of the street along which they drove. The prison was enormous. It was made up of low buildings surrounded by a great expanse of empty concrete, and then a fence, and then a brown field of dead grass; all this, including the field beyond the fence, was lit by floodlights; three or four lights were trained on each object, so that nothing within the bounds of the prison cast a shadow. The entirety of it sat like a minor moon at the edge of the city, casting its prison light into the muddy decrepitude beyond its walls.

They passed through a series of gates and checkpoints; sentries leaned out to talk to MacDougall and Fallow, to shake their hands and offer them cigarettes, which they generally accepted. No papers were presented, and no mention was made of Frank. At last the keeper of the fourth and final checkpoint rolled his gate aside, and the car advanced into the courtyard of the prison, where it was met by a group of guards.

—This is the prisoner? one of them asked. Frank found himself inclined to like the guards at once; they, at least, paid him some attention.

—It is. MacDougall was solemn.

—What was his crime?

—Drawing.

—What was his profession?

—Profession? MacDougall asked Frank.

—Launderer.

—Launderer, MacDougall told the guard.

—Term of incarceration?

—Indefinite.

—Visitors?

—Why not? MacDougall said, and patted Frank on the arm.

—Very good.

MacDougall and Fallow climbed back into their car, and drove as far as the first gate, where they invited the sentry to join them for a drink. Then the gate closed, and Frank was left alone with the guards.

(From Frank's prison notebooks)

Day Eight

THEY WON'T LET ME DRAW. IT'S THE ONE thing I'm not allowed to do. To put pencil to paper in such a way that the result is a drawing. I haven't seen paints anywhere, but I doubt they'd let me paint, either, anyway. So I begin my journal. I've been here a week now. They've assigned me to a cell with three other prisoners, Harris, Brown, and Smith. Their crimes, respectively, are embellishment, smuggling, and juggling. Harris is the embellisher: he sold futures in a real-estate development which seemed so much better than it was that citizens bought in by the thousands; he was caught at the train station with a suitcase full of money and a few pamphlets left over for emergencies. He isn't allowed to refer to anything he can't see, hear, touch, or taste, which limits his conversation somewhat.

Brown smuggled newspapers from one part of the city to another. Not all papers report the same events at the same time, he
explained; by importing papers from the richer parts of town into
the poorer ones (or vice versa), it was sometimes possible to get a
jump on the news, which he could sell to reporters, editors, or
those who make a hobby of betting on current events. He explained that this was a popular pastime in the tenements. It's popular here, too, but Brown can't have anything to do with it. He's
been forbidden to read.

Smith is the juggler. In his prime, he says, he could keep seven
or eight sabers in the air at once. He added to this an equal number of torches, and even kept a pair of balls, he says, bouncing
from one foot to another. He was famous, and played on the
stages of the New Opera and the Old. One night, just after his
wife left him, he had a fit and inadvertently threw four of his
sabers through the necks of as many visiting dignitaries. His punishment seems the hardest: he's been forbidden automatism of all
sorts; he is compelled to perform every action voluntarily. Even
his breathing is watched: a warden visits periodically to check
that it is irregular. —What are you in for? he asked.

I explained to him that I had lost Prudence.

—I suppose that's true of all of us, Harris said.

No one knows what will happen if we do the things we've been
prohibited, but the punishments are apparently quite severe.

We each have our restrictions, and we each have our assignments. Harris works in the infirmary and Smith in the kitchen;
Brown is on the grounds staff and every day goes out with his cart
to collect the birds which collided in the night with the electric

fence. I work in the laundry. It's larger than the laundry at Mrs. Bellaway's, but otherwise just the same, except that I wash prison uniforms instead of judges' robes. At night we have classes. The guards teach us astronomy, anatomy, botany, and mathematics; they teach the prose essay and still life in watercolor (which I'm not allowed to attend), oceanography and animal husbandry, which is largely theoretical. This is a model prison. It is never dark. Lights shine on every corner of the grounds in such a way that there are no shadows. Within the walls it's perpetually noon, and it's only when we are allowed outside that we can see a trace, above us, of day or night. The motto of the prison is BECOME WHAT YOU ARE. It's written everywhere: on plaques in the cells, in the washrooms, over the doors of the refectory. Even above the trough where I wash uniforms there's an inscription, Become What You Arse (the "s" interpolated in pen by another inmate). The guards tell us that each person, inmate or no, has a prisoner within: a struggling mass of potentials, forgotten knowledge, unrealized desires, and unfulfilled ambitions. In becoming what we are, we set the inner prisoner, as it were, free. This is our doctrine. Every morning at six we chant it while doing our calisthenics: Become! What! You! Are! At noon, before we eat, we say it as a grace: May We Become What We Are. And in the evening, when the classes are done, we ask ourselves, What Have We Become? Then we go to sleep in the light and the next morning we begin again.

Your inner prisoner, the guards told me, needs to speak. Let your inner prisoner speak. They gave me a notebook and a pencil. Write in it whatever you want, they said. Don't censor yourself. Let your inner prisoner be your guide. But don't let us

catch you drawing, eh? With that warning they left me, and so
I've begun.

Day Fifteen

To provoke spontaneous self-expression (the expression of our
inner selves, or inner prisoners, that is), the guards give us rest
periods at random. Today we had one in the afternoon, and I
went to the library, to see whether someone else had written a
prison notebook which I could use as a model for my own. The
library has an extensive collection of prison diaries, by well-
known authors—I had no idea that so many writers had spent
some time locked up. For all their variety, however, the books
fall into three general categories: 1) the diary which explains
Why I Am in Prison, and rails against injustice. 2) the diary
which pretends I Am Not in Prison, and goes about fantastic
business; and 3) the diary which describes What I Will Do When
I Get Out of Prison, and plots revolution. I can't write any of
these. I'm here because the police are madmen unchecked by
judges or courts, that's simple enough. I can't pretend that I'm
not in prison, because my business is drawing and I'm not allowed to do it. As for what I'll do when I get out, my term is endless, so: nothing. If I am to keep a notebook at all, it will have to
be of a different sort. It will be called I Am in Prison Forever, and
in it I will teach myself not to draw.

Day Twenty-one

Brown dreamed last night that he was reading a newspaper, and woke us with his crying. We're all fascinated by the future, here. The newspapers in the library are three days old but we read them religiously, although it means sneaking away when we should be doing something else. At night we talk about what we've read and place our bets. I have never known so much about the world. I've learned all about our country's troubles with our neighbors to the east, and how diplomatic relations have ceased; I've learned about the disputed fisheries which are the heart of the matter, and the noxious chemicals which our neighbor has dumped into the water to spite our fishermen. I've learned that the situation is tense. I've learned about the drought in the south, and about the calf-less spring, which perplexed the ranchers on the great plains to the north; about the plays performed in the city's theaters, and the criminals held in custody by the police. Best of all was the news that ancient ruins had been found within the enclosure of the prison. We discussed it at night as though it were the newest thing of all: ancient ruins. Archaeologists say that the ruins may have been an observatory. They say our ancestors may have known more than is generally suspected about the geography of the moon. There was a picture in the newspaper of a stone disk unearthed by the diggers. It was broken in places, and parts of it were missing; the surface of the disk was covered with marks which might have been writing. A Map of the Moon? the caption read. Odds that the caption was correct were set at three to seven.

We discuss in order to make odds. We make odds so that we can bet. We bet the money which we will have when we are released. Elaborate accounts are kept on chits of paper, which we hide in our mattresses and in the drains of our broken sinks. Everyone bets except a few who abstain on principle, and Brown who isn't allowed to read, and Harris who isn't allowed to speak of possibilities, of course. Even the ones who, like me, are here forever, find a way to make bets. We bet the money of our loved ones, our families, our children, if we have any. We sign promissory notes enjoining our heirs to pay such-and-such a sum to our fellow inmates upon their release. Because no money actually changes hands, the odds are very great. We bet on the most improbable events. The odds that the guards will turn to doves and fly off? Fifty thousand to one. And there are takers. The odds that there will be a war with the country to the east: three to one. The odds that we'll be drafted: five to one. The odds that the other country will win, and we'll be released: a thousand to one, but falling. There are even bets, which have been standing for years now, on metaphysical events. The odds that the soul is immortal have been calculated, along with the odds for and against the existence of God. I don't remember the numbers, but it doesn't seem to me that very many people have bet on the soul.

Day Twenty-eight

Because I have been here for a month, I am allowed visitors. James and Rosalyn came; we sat on opposite sides of a glass partition and spoke to one another through a grille. James told me that he has taken over my job at Mrs. Bellaway's. He told Mrs. Bellaway that I'd gone on a trip, so she wouldn't think that he associated with criminals. He looked tired; I'm afraid that the work doesn't suit him. Rosalyn washes dishes in the boardinghouse kitchen. They've stayed on in my room. My easel, my charcoal, my inks and sketchbooks are gone, confiscated by the police for evidentiary purposes. A few visitors looked for me in the days following the arrest, then the visits stopped. Bonnie has not been by, nor Ernest. I have received no mail. Mrs. Bellaway mentions me only as a standard to fault James's work. She speaks of me as though I had lived in the boardinghouse years ago and had since gone on to greater things. James and Rosalyn told me that they were glad to see me all the same.

—You look so thin, though, Rosalyn said. What do they make you do?

—The laundry. I wash our uniforms and learn about anatomy and the stars.

James and Rosalyn nodded, not quite understanding, but impressed by the strangeness of the prison regime. They looked as though they were afraid to ask the obvious questions: am I beaten (no); is the discipline harsh (yes); have I made any plans to escape (no); and what's it like to live in the company of career criminals (not that different from anywhere else). I asked them for news. But James knew nothing about the disputed fisheries, or the war brewing with our neighbor to the east, or the drought, or the ancient ruins. He told me that a pestilence had broken out in the parts of the city reclaimed from the marsh: the limbs of those afflicted became arthritic, then calcified, then turned to ash and blew away. Doctors are working on a vaccine.

That was all we had time for. Looking back as the guard led me off, I could see them brushing their fingertips against the surface of the glass, as though they couldn't believe that this was what separated them from prison, this transparent sheet, this nothing.

Day Eighty-four

Last night Smith was caught breathing evenly in his sleep. He was taken away and transferred elsewhere. These things happen in the prison all the time—the old prisoners say it happens most often while we sleep, so that no one will complain. The nature of the punishment inflicted on those taken away is, like everything else, the subject of numerous bets. Some say that the prisoners are killed, and some that they are merely changed beyond recognition. Others say that they are removed to an even larger prison, where they wander without the benefit of guards, assignments, or restrictions, and that this is the worst punishment of all.

Our new cellmate is Jones, a voyeur, forbidden to look at other people. He keeps, understandably, to himself.

Day One Hundred and Ninety-six

James and Rosalyn came today in a state of agitation.

—Frank! James leaned close to the glass. —You've been discovered.

By one of the coincidences that are apparently not uncommon in the city, a great collector of art, on his way home from a studio in one of the young neighborhoods of converted garages and

water towers, caught sight of a poster I'd drawn. It was the one
of the uncle whose nephew had a better memory for character
than for appearance; he could tell me only that his vanished rel-
ative had been garrulous, prejudiced against groups but willing
to make exceptions for individuals, hardworking, afraid of death,
overfond of cologne. Something about the poster held the collector's interest. He took it down and showed it to his friends,
who were similarly intrigued; more posters were sought, and
found, mostly in the suburbs (where posters are only infrequently defaced) and in the parts of the city where the police
(who had been instructed to remove all my work) rarely go except on more serious business. The collector brought the posters
to the owner of a gallery, who agreed to mount an exhibition. A
critic came to the opening, and mentioned it to a friend, a curator of the Isinglass Museum, infamous for its retrospectives. The
curator visited the gallery and bought all my known work, with
an option to buy any pieces which might turn up at a later date.
My posters were given their own room in the museum. At first
they were seen only by those who, having got lost, were happy
to find a comfortable bench to rest on before finding their way
out again. After a disoriented columnist for the city's serious
newspaper sat there, however, a long review was printed, and the
posters moved closer to the museum's entrance.

—Here it is, James said, and took a folded page from his
pocket. Listen: "The painter's works have all the freshness of a
death mask, capturing pain at the moment of its cessation, and
grief before it has properly begun. One wonders whether Hugo,
whose life remains one of the mysteries of our time, found his
subjects among the mad, or whether he was one of those young

draftsmen who haunt the morgues, hoping to emulate the Old Masters whose genius lay in their intuition for the forms of the dead."

—Hugo? I asked.

—It's your pseudonym. Taken from the poster of the uncle.

—But I couldn't draw the dead.

—Never mind that. He says such wonderful things! Like this: "Hugo's lines have the certainty of life itself. To look at the *Portrait of Saul*"—listen, portrait of Saul, doesn't that sound, well, solid—anyway, to look at it "is to feel oneself submerged in a meticulous psychology of appearances, which can allow no detail that does not betray something of the subject's past. Clearly *Saul* is the work of an old man, near himself to death, and thus cognizant of the full weight of life that has already begun to oppress the schoolboy. We have, in short, not to deal with pictures so much as with people, although they are people whom one would perhaps not like to meet, would not dare even to meet, and this constitutes the nucleus of Hugo's genius: to introduce us to a world in which we are not at home, which is nevertheless recognizably our own. Here one would like to speculate as to the life of the painter, his childhood amid the bustle of the docks and his apprenticeship in the towers of the Painting School, his eventual madness and slow, brilliant decline, like a candle that gives off strange colors as it gutters. But in the end one must be thankful for Hugo's anonymity, which is different in degree perhaps but not in kind from the mystery that descends upon any work of art at the moment of its completion." That's beautiful, isn't it, Frank?

—I'm not sure.

—I'm going to write to him, and tell him that it's you, not Hugo, who made the posters, that you're still alive, that you're young. You could draw a hundred more of those, and think! They'd pay you a thousand dollars for each one, or more, you'd be rich, Frank.

—I'm rich already.

—What?

—Never mind.

How could I explain, with the guards listening, that the odds against the limb-calcifying plague had been set at four thousand nine hundred and seventy to one?

—They'll have to let you out of prison, when you're famous. There'll be a scandal, and the Mayor in person will write your pardon. We'll buy a house, not a mansion, but something with a real studio for you up in the hills, and we'll put up a fence around it to keep the reporters away.

—Don't write. The Mayor won't believe you.

—I'm your friend, Frank. I can't just sit by and watch.

—It won't do any good.

—I can try. Don't you want to get out of prison?

—Even if he believes you, it won't matter. They won't let me out. I've been sentenced to perpetuity.

—At least I can set things straight, so they know it's you, not Hugo. And you can draw portraits from prison? *Frank's Prison Sketchbooks*, we'll call them. I'll be your distributor.

—It's no use, and anyway we become what we are. Do you have any other news?

Day One Thousand and Eight

So this is what perpetuity is like. I would have expected it to pass more slowly. I've learned the parts of the eye and the names of distant galaxies, the breadth of the ocean and the height of the southern mountains. I've become immensely rich in prison money, at first with the tips I got from James and Rosalyn, and then, when they stopped coming, with some carefully placed bets of my own. My strategy is to encourage the hopes of others, and then bet against them. I get a little money from each one, and over time it adds up. There was a war; no one won and we were not released; the guards haven't turned into doves. Each time I make a few dollars.

Today, while I was eating, a boy sat down beside me. He looked no older than fourteen or fifteen; I wondered what crime he'd committed to be locked up so young. He whispered:
—The prison is destroyed by the ocean, and the guards drown. All the prisoners who survive are freed. Two million to one. Want it?
—Sure. That's the kind of bet I like.
I was curious, though, how the youth had managed to think up something so improbable on his own. Usually I have to make up the long shots, then convince the hopeful ones to bet on them.
—You make that one up yourself?
—No sir. It was Orestes.
—Who's he?
—My cellmate. He's always thinking of things like that.
—And you believe him?
—Enough to bet a dollar anyway.

—What about ten dollars? That's twenty million, if you win.

—You haven't got twenty million.

—Want to bet?

—Okay, ten dollars.

—What else does Orestes tell you?

—Oh, all sorts of things. For instance, he says you're in love with a photographer named Prudence.

I hadn't heard the name in so long, and expected so little to hear it in the prison refectory, that for a moment I thought he must be talking about someone else.

—Orestes says he knows where she went.

—What? Where?

The boy smirked. —It's a long story.

I pressed him to tell me, but he insisted that only Orestes could do the story justice.

—Where do I find him, then?

—I can't say. The boy lowered his voice. —You see, I'm not allowed to give directions.

—Tell me, or the bet's off.

The boy looked around. —I'll tell you what. I'll draw you a map. But first . . . He made out a wager chit for me to sign. Ten dollars stake, odds two million to one, return twenty million dollars. That was all the money I had, maybe a little more. I signed.

—Have you got a piece of paper?

I gave him this notebook. He opened to a fresh page and began to draw. A moment later, a passing guard seized him by the collar and dragged him out of the refectory.

If only he had time to finish the map! As it is, all I can see is that Orestes's cell is far away, practically on the other side of the prison—but is that circle the central watchtower or the reservoir? No one in the refectory or elsewhere has heard of him, except for Brown, who remembers a prisoner named Orestes but thinks he died long ago.

All my lines lead nowhere.

Day One Thousand and Fifteen

A rest day. In the library as usual, but the papers have nothing worth betting on. The weather is fair, and the threat of another war distant. I was surprised to read that Max, from Bonnie's salon, was arrested for seditious activities—perhaps I'll see him here soon.

The boy, damn him, got me thinking about Prudence again. For a long time I had been able not to think about her—nothing reminds me of her here, where the city's visible only as a line of darkness above and beyond the outer wall—but she's come into my thoughts again. I think of her as I wash uniforms, in evening classes, at night when the guards walk slowly from one cell to another, making sure that we are in bed, but not too soundly asleep. I see her face—I see your face, Prudence, why not write to you? as clearly as I ever saw it when you sat for a portrait. I think I could draw you now. And why not? The guards don't care what I do. They used to look over my shoulder sometimes, when I was writing, to make sure that no drawing stole onto the page. While I worked in the laundry, they opened my cell and leafed through my notebook. They know I'm no sort of artist any longer. Yet sometimes, in our classes, my hand of its own accord fills the mar-

P A U L   L A F A R G E

gins of my notebook with geometric designs, and the guards pay
no attention. One night at dinner I drew Harris's face in a puddle
of brown sauce, and wiped it clean with a spoon. The guards
didn't come, but if they had I think they would have been
amused: I got his beak just right, and the disagreement of his eyebrows, which wriggle at each other like dueling inchworms. I
breathe on a cold windowpane in the library, and trace faces in
the fogged glass with my fingertip, and no one comes. The room
is empty except for the old librarian, who reads the newspaper.
He bets with the prisoners, and shrewdly: some say that he's the
richest man in the prison, not excepting the warden and all the
guards. He can see my notebook, but not what I write in it—and
if he could see, would he tell? I don't think so: he's made good
money betting with me, and we have a few bets unsettled. I could
draw you, Prudence, I will draw you, and perhaps I'll forget you,
perhaps I won't have to think of you every day between now and
the end of perpetuity.

(Here Frank's prison notebooks end.)

THE GUARDS LED HIM PAST SHELVES DE-
voted to comparative dentistry and uni-
versal languages, to the part of the library
where old periodicals were kept. Frank
had never been there before—why would
he? all those bets were settled long ago—
and he was surprised to see, beyond it, a
second reading room, smaller than the
first but more comfortably appointed,
with armchairs and low lamps awaiting
the readers' pleasure.

—I'm afraid there's been some mistake,
Frank said.

—You all say that, replied an old
guard. —But we know when you've
cracked.

—I didn't draw anything, though.

—Oh? The guard took Frank's notebook and turned to the half-finished map.
—What's this, then?

—But—

—Not that we hold it against you. You
become what you become, and there's

nothing we can do about it. Never mind that we work ourselves half to death for your benefit.

The guards stopped at a metal door in the library's rear wall. One of them leafed through a ring of keys, and another struggled to pull back a rusty bolt.

—What are you going to do to me? Frank asked.

—Do? Why, nothing. We're setting you free. But first there's the matter of your debt.

The guard extracted an official-looking document from the breast pocket of his uniform. —Don't you feel that you owe something, just a token, if you want, to those who've treated you so well?

The document gave the prison, or rather its staff, title to Frank's estate, and the right to collect from all those who owed him money, present and future. All it needed was a signature, and as Frank finished reading, the guard handed him a pencil. —It's the least you can do.

The guards had got the door open. On the other side was darkness. Was it night outside the prison?

Frank signed.

—Now I can leave?

—Who said anything about leaving? Free is entirely different, and, if you want my opinion, infinitely more valuable. We could let you go, of course we could: in fifteen minutes you could be on Promontory Street admiring the ladies, but would you be free? The old guard looked as though he were about to say something more, but his comrades had lost patience. One of them gave Frank a lazy shove, and he fell headlong through the door. Pale spires and rooftops rushed toward him, then Frank struck his head, and saw nothing at all.

Slowly the darkness thinned to a gray obscurity in which the outlines of things were visible, but not their colors. Frank learned to discern shade and deeper shade, and the world regained some of its depth, although its extent was, for the time being, unknowable. He lay on his chest on a rough floor of stone or ill-poured concrete, between the brick façade of a townhouse and the embossed doors of a dwarfish cathedral. Ahead of him, a stone gate rose into the gloom; beyond it, Frank made out a row of fashionable houses, a store window, a sort of domed gazebo which might have been an observatory. It was as though all the elements of the city above had been shaken in a giant's cup and tossed haphazardly into the cellar, with hardly enough room for a person to squeeze between them. Frank stood up groggily and rapped on the cathedral door. The whole building shook, or rather the whole façade: the rest of the cathedral was missing. The fashionable house opposite was even less real: only the painting of a house, although so cleverly done that the illusion wasn't apparent until Frank's nose brushed the canvas.

He wondered what sort of world he'd fallen into. Here was a police detective's office, furnished with posters of wanted criminals; here a cottage, a barbershop, a potter's wheel. The country too had its place in the gloom: hillsides and orchards, forests bisected by streams, plains and distant mountains all figured in the jumble, often in impossible proximity to one another, like a landscape seen through a kaleidoscope. Half the scenery—

the mountains, the stream—was only painted canvas; the other—
the trees and bushes, a windmill—was solid, though lifeless.
The fruit did not come off the trees. In the shadow of an inn,
whose front steps at least were real, Frank stumbled over a small
form which cried out, —Ow! Can't you look where you're
going?

A silhouette rose to its feet, and Frank recognized the boy who
had bet him that the prison would be destroyed by the ocean.

—Well, if it isn't the gambler. Have you just come in?

Frank nodded. —Listen, I'm sorry . . .

—Never mind that now. Have you got anything to eat?

—No.

—Pity. The boy sighed and sat down, as if deflated, on the
steps.

—Where are we? Frank asked.

—Can't you guess? This is where they keep the extras. Everything they—he pointed his thumb at the ceiling—don't need,
they keep here until they want it again.

—You mean this stuff is all from the prison?

—Not just from prison, it's everything. Everything no one
wants.

—That's ridiculous. For one thing, it wouldn't all fit down
here.

—That's what I thought at first, too. But then I figured out
their system. When they want to bring something big in, a house,
say, they take the air out first, so it's all flat. And when they want
the house back again, pssht! They blow it up and it's good as new.

The boy's brain must have been addled by his fall into the cellar, Frank thought. Although in truth his hypothesis was no

stranger than Prudence's story about the Found Objects Bureau. Frank's head ached. Of course the Bureau was only a story. How could anyone, even the police, collect everything the city lost? The truth was that all those things went nowhere. Or rather that each lost thing went to a different place. Probably the same was true of the missing.

The boy kicked a small, shiny object out of a corner. It skittered to a stop by Frank's feet: a brooch, wrought in such a way that if the light caught it one way, you saw a face in profile; if the other, the crescent moon.

—Rubbish, the boy said. Stuff like that comes in all the time. You're sure you haven't got anything to eat?

Frank turned the brooch over. An inscription was engraved on the back: WELCOME HOME ELISE, and a date long past.

—Some bread, or chocolate, or anything at all?

—Don't they feed you down here?

—Oh, sure, sometimes when the buildings come back in there's a piece of bread or a pear or something like that inside which someone left behind, but it's not what you'd call regular eating.

—What do you live on, then?

The boy looked at Frank coolly. —You're down here too, you know. No use pretending you're not.

Frank put the brooch in his pocket and turned to go. Before he'd got far, however, the boy called out, —Wait! I'm coming, and tottered after Frank on legs thin as stilts, and as unsteady.

The boy, whose name was Comio, told Frank that prisoners were dumped in the cellar at the rate of two or three a day, but if that was true, then the cellar must have been very large, for they met no one at all. Only now and then, as they wandered between the buildings, Frank thought he saw a face watching them from a glassless window, from between the slats of a fence, from under a canvas painted to look like a mountainside. When he called out, each face retreated as though it had been slapped, and did not reappear. —Don't they want to talk? Frank asked. —Maybe they've been down here too long, and know better, Comio said, but refused to explain what he meant by it. He prowled in and out of the rooms; now and then he brought Frank a glass of water or a half-eaten sandwich. —Got to keep you alive, he said, or how will I collect on my bet?

Frank considered telling him about the paper he'd signed, which had made him a pauper again. As it seemed unlikely that either one of them would live to see the terms of their bet fulfilled, however, he kept quiet and let Comio tell him, endlessly, how he would spend his winnings, when he'd left the prison behind once and for all. —I'll have a different car for every day of the week, the boy said, and a house for each car, and a wife for each house. Frank wondered what the wives would think of this arrangement, but Comio had an answer ready: —How could they complain, when they'll each have a house and a car to themselves six days a week? He went on to describe the decoration of each house, and became very detailed; Frank's attention wandered.

—Orestes says the ocean's coming soon, Comio concluded.

—Says? Is he down here, too?

—He came with me.

—Why?

—His punishment: he's not allowed to be alone.

They passed a stone head as tall as a man. Its narrow, chiseled face grinned fiercely, as though it had just perpetrated some amusing act of savagery.

—Where is he now, then?

—Oh, not far away.

—Alone?

—Well. Comio shrugged. —What are they going to do? He's already here.

—Can I see him?

—If you want. But you can't call the bet off now: you signed.

They found Orestes in the replica of a prison cell—complete in every detail except the bars—snoring on the bottom bunk. Instead of the usual prison smock, he wore a night-blue uniform with silver buttons, like a guard's, which gave Frank occasion to wonder whether one's inner prisoner might not be watched by an inner jailer, who grew stronger, too, in his own way, over time.

Comio shook the sleeper. —Time to get up, old man.

—What! he screeched. Is it the end? Fire or flood?

—You've got a visitor.

Orestes rubbed his puffed-up eyes and smiled, showing two good teeth and as many bad ones. —Who are you?

—A friend of Comio's. That is, we had a bet—

—I never bet. Either I know things, or I don't know them. If I know them, then they're certain. If they're certain, then it's not right to bet.

—You told him that I was in love with a photographer named Prudence.

Orestes blinked.

—He said you know where she went.

—Do I? There are so many stories, I can't tell one from another anymore.

—Try to remember. Take your time. Frank gestured at the cell and the darkness beyond. —I'm not going anywhere.

—That's what it's like, being old. You don't forget anything; you just can't tell it apart from anything else. Fortunately, it's all connected, somehow. A prisoner in love . . . Well, there's Maurice.

—Who?

—One of the very first prisoners. He was a vegetable seller by trade, but during the war—

—Never mind about that. Where's Prudence?

— . . . he lost everything but sleep; then he lost that, too.

—Where is she?

—Of course that sort of thing happens in prison all the time. Since Maurice's time, though—

—I don't care about Maurice. I want to know—

—Ssh! What did I just tell you, gambler? It's all the same story.

The Prisoner Who Dreamed of Fish

Long ago, when the prison was young, it was not as it is today. It was nothing but a low stone hall, divided into cells with barred windows and barred doors and a warden, an old man, who smoked a pipe and threw food in to the prisoners through the door or through the windows, depending on his mood. He never talked to them about self-improvement, and never let them out for air or exercise, for he was a cruel old man, and the thought of the prisoners languishing in darkness while he walked freely past their cells gave him great pleasure. I say walked, but in fact he clopped: the warden had a wooden leg, and when he tired of walking he would unstrap the leg and strike the bars of the cells with his false limb. In this way he prevented the prisoners from sleeping, because the warden was an insomniac in addition to being cruel, and he couldn't stand the thought that his charges might have any peace which was denied to him. He struck one cell and then another, banged until he heard the prisoner wake, and cry as he came slowly out of whatever dream he'd been lost in, and remembered again that he was a prisoner, and a poor, abused prisoner at that. Not one of them was allowed to sleep through the night. Most, however, were only awakened once or twice, because more often than not the warden struck on the same door, so regularly that the unlucky occupant of that cell never had more than fifteen minutes' rest at a time. The warden was cruel to all the prisoners, but to this one most of all. He gave him the last of the food, which on most days was nothing more than scrapings from the pot in which the prison gruel was prepared. Sometimes the warden threw the food upwards into the cell with great violence, so that the prisoner had to jump up and scrape it off the ceiling with his fingers; sometimes he rolled the food in dirt, and sometimes did not feed the prisoner at all, but gave each of the other inmates a little extra.

The warden was cruel on account of his daughter, whose name was June. She visited the prison once a week to wash the prisoners' linen, mend their clothes, and minister to their cuts and sores, which would otherwise have killed them, for the prison was not a clean place. June felt sympathy for the prisoners because she,

too, was a sort of captive, kept at home all week long and allowed
out only to visit the prison, so that the inmates wouldn't all die
and the warden thereby lose his salary. Maurice, however, was
her favorite, because he was handsome and always asleep. The
other prisoners frightened her; they looked at her in ways which,
even as a girl, she understood very well. Maurice alone did not
stare; in fact, he slept through her first visits, waking only to rise
from his bed so that it could be stripped of its sheet, then falling
again onto the straw, asleep as soundly as if he had never moved.
The other prisoners were always begging for one thing or another; only Maurice asked her for nothing, so the warden's
daughter scoured his sheet so that it was spotless, and rubbed it
with rough stones to make the cloth more supple; she mended his
pillowcase and stuffed fistfuls of feathers into his pillow. She
sewed a warm lining into his prison smock and darned his socks,
so that neither cold nor discomfort might disturb the perfection
of his sleep. June knew that it was perfect, and that her work
could do nothing to improve it, but she hoped that the softness of
his pillow and the warmth of his smock would register in Maurice's dreams, and that he might wonder, in his sleep, who had
been so kind to him. At first her work seemed to have no effect.
Maurice slept blissfully when she arrived, and hardly opened an
eye during the entire length of her visit. Once, when she was
preparing to leave, he woke up and ambled sleepily to the door of
his cell, where he blinked at her, turned around, and fell asleep on
the floor. The next week, when June came into his cell again, she
thought his eyes were only half-closed. He mumbled in his sleep:
was it her name? Little by little she fell in love with him entirely.
She was careful to conceal her love from the warden, who was, as

I've said, jealous of her. She never washed Maurice's sheets when her father was looking, and made sure that his back was turned before she went into Maurice's cell. The warden, who watched her carefully as she ministered to the highwaymen and desperadoes, left her alone with Maurice, whom he found ridiculous, effeminate, and altogether not a respectable criminal. One day, as he passed the open door of Maurice's cell, the warden saw his daughter bent forward over the prisoner, her lips pressed almost to his cheek. He thought that they had kissed, but he was wrong: in fact, June was whispering her name over and over, to ensure that it was received into her lover's sleep. June! The warden shouted, and clopped into the cell, where he beat his daughter a little.

Maurice woke up. It was the first time in all his confinement that he had been thoroughly awake; he had trained himself early on to sleep through the things which necessitated his getting out of bed: the eating and the pissing and the weekly changing of the sheet. What was more, it was the first time he had been even remotely conscious of the warden's daughter. Whatever June thought she had heard him mumble was, in fact, something altogether different. Maurice dreamed of fish. He drifted on the water in a little boat, dangling a line over the side and occasionally pulling fantastic pink fish with the faces of men into the boat, where he talked with them for a while, then threw them back into the ocean. He dreamed of fish stories: the oldest fish told him about the time when there had been land, and things alive on it, mountains and islands and green horizons; the fish told him how beasts had moved through the air—just so, they said, flapping— and of the strange objects they had found in the water: bits of wood carved in the shape of fish, bubbles of shiny glass, lengths of line and fallen kites and the unhappy men whom they had dragged into the water, those wise fish with the faces of men. They told Maurice of the disturbances of the moon, which sometimes drew very close to the earth, and sometimes retreated to a great distance, so that it was hardly larger than the evening stars. Once the moon had provoked great tides, and set the bottom of the ocean all astir; the fish told him how, from a safe distance, they had bobbed atop the waves and watched the ocean cover the land, first the sandy coasts and then the forests, the smaller islands which sank all at once with a sucking noise, and the larger ones which subsided slowly, tilting this way and that, and settling finally into the water, so that only a mountain or two remained; then the tide rose again and the mountains sank.

These were the things Maurice dreamed about, and in truth he had forgotten that such a thing as land still existed; so, when he woke up, he was surprised to find himself on it, and to find it all around him. Then Maurice saw June and the warden, June being beaten by the warden, in his own cell, and he cried out, mistaking the warden for a fisherman and June, thrashing, for his catch; he picked the warden up by the nape of his neck and threw him, peg leg and all, into the corridor. Maurice's sympathy was with the fish. June, who was startled and more than a bit upset, ran out of the cell, too, and before she knew it the warden had slammed the cell door shut and begun to beat her again.

That was the end of Maurice's sleep. Too agitated to lie down, he shook the bars of his cell and watched June as she was sent off to do her mending elsewhere. He watched as the warden came back and, for the first time, unstrapped his wooden leg and made the bars of his cell ring. He drummed on the doors of the other cells, too, for he had found a new way of being cruel, and in general, once he had found a way of being cruel, he stuck with it. So Maurice lost his dreams. No sooner did he get his bearings, and lay his line over the side of his boat, than the warden returned to rattle the bars of his cell. Maurice missed his conversations with the fish more than anything about his life before prison. In fact, he had trouble remembering what it had been like not to be in prison. He thought it must have something to do with dance halls, and keeping accounts, and the buying and selling of vegetables, but imagined these things only vaguely, as though they belonged to a world which had been submerged.

Maurice had sold vegetables, he was right about that. He was imprisoned because he'd been careless about his accounts (he liked to spend his nights in dance halls), and, with a simple arithmetical error, he'd overcharged the Navy commissariat by a factor of ten for a boatload of turnips, and this at a time when the outcome of the war was in doubt and provisions in short supply. When the error was discovered, after the war had been settled, Maurice was imprisoned for profiteering. He fell asleep on the very first day of his captivity. He slept for three years before June found him, and was awake for the three years that followed. In this second epoch Maurice's thoughts grew more and more confused. At first he tried to console himself by telling the fishes' stories to the other prisoners, in a whisper, when the warden was napping; but the others wouldn't listen, and he was stuck telling the stories to himself. He told them over and over, and eventually wrote them, or rather carved them, in the floor of his cell, with a sharp-edged spoon. The warden yelled and banged on the bars, but couldn't stop Maurice from carving, except by going into the cell himself, which he was afraid to do. When all the stories had been written, Maurice tried to make up new ones: he began a story about an old fisherman who pulled a fish with June's face from the sea, but it ended with the fisherman cooking and eating the fish, and this was an ending Maurice preferred not to record. He invented a story about a young vegetable dealer, horribly wronged, who sails across an ocean, becomes rich, and returns, to the great chagrin of those who wronged him, but the only scenes for which he had any real enthusiasm were those which took place on the ocean, and so the story had neither a beginning nor an end, but only a vast, watery middle. By the end of the third year he no longer made up stories, but sat on his pallet, muttering unconnected words: *kite, tide, dock, ebb,* again and again. The warden was delighted. He didn't need to drag his leg across the bars of Maurice's cell anymore; even when he was busy elsewhere, the muttering continued, as though Maurice had forgotten how to sleep. The warden liked to pass his nights in front of that cell; he would draw his chair up close and sit with his head cocked, listening to the words which followed one another without so much as a conjunction between them.

I hardly have to tell you that June wasn't allowed back in the prison. A deaf-mute was engaged to collect the inmates' things and carry them in a basket to the warden's house, where June had become a prisoner in all but name. At the end of the third year since his awakening, Maurice remembered the fish—or no, the woman—who appeared once in his cell (so he thought) and never again. In the confused world of broken-down stories which he had come to live in, it seemed to him that there had been no dream and no waking, only a simple metamorphosis of fish into woman. Maurice marveled at the warden's power, for he had killed his fish more thoroughly than fish was ever killed with hook and line. But this was perhaps not the right way to understand the end of his dream. He had seen June dragged away, and said so to himself for days: dragged, dragged, dragged. The warden wondered what he was thinking now, and hoped that Maurice's death would soon follow the reduction of his vocabulary to a single word. Dragged, dragged, Maurice thought, but to where? That was the question. A conviction had begun to form itself in Maurice's mind, which anyone who had slept for more than a few minutes in three years would have taken for love: he believed that all would be well if only he could find June again. Maurice was not, despite appearances, altogether mad: he knew that the deaf-mute who disturbed him once a week had taken the place of the pretty laundress. He crushed the tiny insects which lived in great numbers in his cell, and with their acidic juices spelled out a simple message on the inside of his pillowcase, without much hope that it would ever be seen: Come, it read, to my window.

June, I should say, had not stopped thinking about her somnolescent lover since the day when she was sent away from the jail. Lovers grow to be like what they love, and June was no exception: she slept for as many as sixteen hours a day, hoping to find Maurice in her sleep. She grew paler, and softer, and her eyes blinked irritably in the light; when she was not asleep she washed the prisoners' smocks and composed long poems which, she hoped, captured the lovely shadows which ran from her memory each time her father came to wake her up. She found Maurice's message at once, being the sort of person who turns pillowcases inside out before washing them. That night June feigned sleep until the house was entirely still; then she rose and went outside. The moon was bright, and she found her way easily to the prison, which was just where it is now, between the city and the ocean. She stole past the single guard, and in no time she stood by the window of Maurice's cell, where she brushed her fingers against the bars, a gesture she'd unwittingly inherited from her father. In a moment Maurice's fingers took hold of hers, and she nearly cried out with joy—but restrained herself, and fortunately, for the warden slept in a chair just outside Maurice's cell. Maurice smiled at June through the bars, and murmured, Drown, drown, over and over. Drown. The warden woke up, heard this new word, and watched Maurice carefully. The prisoner looked sincere; he stood at the window of his cell, holding the bars weakly, thin enough and frail enough that the warden wondered if he would even be able to reach the ocean unassisted. Drown, Maurice said, drown drown drown, until the warden had no doubt he would do it, given the opportunity. It wouldn't be hard to make it look like an accident. The locks on the doors of the cells were old; they hadn't been replaced in all the warden's tenure, which went back so far that even the oldest prisoners could not remember his predecessor. He could break the lock, and say the prisoner did it; then he would lead Maurice to the ocean and be troubled by him no more. The warden rubbed his hands with delight, unstrapped his leg, and banged on the lock to Maurice's cell. June, just outside the window, marveled at the intelligence of this scheme. Soon the cell was open—and at once Maurice jumped out, grabbed the warden's leg, and stunned him with it; he had at least enough strength for that.

The warden was unconscious for some time. When he opened his eyes again, his head felt as though it had been buffeted by a tremendous wind, and the cell before him was empty. He ran out of the prison. There, in the moonlight, he saw Maurice standing at the water's edge, bending into the waves, his arms extended as though he were about to crouch on all fours. He's really going to do it, the warden thought, and hopped as quickly as he could across the dunes. When he got closer, though, he saw that Maurice was not drowning himself but someone else: long hair rose and fell on the foam, and pale, soft limbs flopped heavily when the waves receded. It was June, of course, and she had not become a fish as Maurice had hoped she would. When the warden saw what had happened, he screamed for the night watch, who came running and dragged Maurice back to his cell. The warden reported June's murder as best he could to the superintendent of prisons, and it was decided that Maurice should be put to death. They led him out of the cell the next morning, they stood him against a wall and shot him, and all this happened without his knowing it, for as soon as June's head had ceased to rise up from the water, he fell asleep, and slept through his own execution.

After that, the prison fell into disrepair, and a new one was built on the same spot; when that one became too small, this one was built here, where Maurice dreamed of fish, and June of him. The guards say that there have been no executions since Maurice's, but I've heard that since then criminals have been put to death at random, to satisfy the old warden, who could after all get no satisfaction from the shooting of a prisoner who was dreaming of fish.

·   ·   ·

—But that's not the end of it, Frank said, confused.

—Why not? It was the end of Maurice.

—What does it have to do with Prudence?

—I don't know what you're talking about.

—Comio said . . .

—The boy's an inveterate liar.

—That's not so! Comio protested.

—Do you know what he's in here for? Disingenuousness.

—What? Frank and Comio said at once.

—He's not as young as he looks.

Comio shook Orestes violently by the shoulders. —Finish the
story, old man.

—All right, all right. Orestes leaned forward and whispered, I
found the stone Maurice carved.

—What?

He explained: The ancient ruins Frank had read about, years
ago, weren't an observatory at all, but the stone in which Maurice
carved the stories told to him by the man-faced fish. From the
photographs in the newspaper, Orestes, who had a gift for ancient
languages, was able to decipher them.

—So I learned that the moon is not even in its orbit, Orestes
said. Now and then it draws close enough to see the earth, and the
earth, inevitably, suffers. The fish, whose lives were governed by
the tide, had developed a science for calculating these disturbances. They taught this science to Maurice, who recorded it on
the stone. It predicts that there will soon be a disturbance. Or that
a disturbance has recently occurred, I don't know which. But the
former seems more likely.

—But the fish were only a dream, said Frank.

—Science is often revealed in dreams.

—And even the dream was only part of a story.

—Stories are good indicators of disaster.

—And what does any of it have to do with Prudence? You don't know where she went, any more than I do.

—Where she went? Of course I know. She went away.

—That's not an answer.

—It's the only answer there is. Now go, gambler. You disgust me.

As the light did not change, it was impossible to mark the progress of time, just as it had been in the prison above. Without meals or classes or work Frank didn't know whether he'd wandered for hours or days. Hunger whispered to him, then nagged, then roared, so that his ears rang. To distract himself, he tried to measure the extent of the cellar, but found that it was impossible to walk in a straight line from one side to the other. It couldn't be that big, though, he decided, nor were there as many buildings in it as there had seemed at first. Rather, they were cleverly designed to serve several purposes at once, so that the low, half-timbered façade which, on the outside, belonged to a country cottage was on the inside a stone-walled dungeon complete with iron sconces (but no lamps) and stains on the floor. Frank wondered whether faces were like that, too. He thought about the ones he'd seen, but could remember nothing exactly, nor keep anything straight. Prudence's features blurred with Evelyn's, with Ernest's, with the imagined face of the June in Orestes's story and the face of the girl, June, who had told him what going south meant, a long time ago.

His hunger abated for a while; then it spoke to him again, in a quiet but insistent voice, assuring him that everything he'd felt thus far had been only a joke, like a clown aping a hungry person. Now, however, the hunger assured him that it was perfectly serious, and would not leave until it was satisfied. Frank prowled in and out of such buildings as could be entered; but without Comio to help him, he found nothing. He walked until his legs were weak, then sat down at the base of a clock tower to rest. Why look farther? Prudence wasn't in the cellar, nor anywhere he could get to—even if the guards were to let him out of the cellar, even if they fed him and set him free, how would he find her, then? Each step he had taken, looking for her, had led him farther from their real, brief union. Prudence became a portrait of Prudence, many portraits, portraits of countless missing people, became words in a prison notebook, rubbish on a prison floor, an old man's babbling about fish and the moon. Orestes was right about one thing: the only place the missing went was away. There was no island off the coast which surfaced at low tide, or if there was, it was empty, uninhabitable. Wherever Prudence was, he would not find her; nor would he look. Frank was done looking. He had become what he was; his inner prisoner corresponded exactly to himself.

Frank remembered how Prudence had taken a picture of the street where Saul had disappeared. He understood, now, what that picture must have shown. Nothing. Without a body, without even a weapon, there was no evidence that a crime had taken place. You could no more take a photograph of the missing than you could draw the dead. Had Prudence understood that? Probably she had not. She doubted her talent already; probably she took the pictures as evidence that it had failed her altogether. No wonder she had gone away. If only Frank hadn't told her about the missing! She might never have seen what was not in her pictures; she might be with him still. The thought that he had somehow caused Prudence's departure filled Frank with a despair so keen and full that it might have passed as any emotion, the way a drowning man might mistake the ocean for a bathtub, or vice versa. He closed his eyes.

Prudence passed by in the darkness, not far off. She wore a camera around her neck, and cupped rolls of film in her hands. June—Frank's June—walked beside her, twirling a stalk of wheat. Bonnie followed, dabbing at her eyes with a handkerchief; then came James, with a guitar, and Rosalyn, her hands folded on her chest like a penitent's. Evelyn and Ernest and Mrs. Bellaway arrived, and each made a little curtsy in Frank's direction as she passed. Then came an assortment of guards and prisoners, bus drivers and transients and members of the salon. —Prudence! Frank called out, but his voice was weak from thirst. She did not see him, but kept walking, turned a corner, and vanished between a country chapel and a gamblers' den. June followed; then, one by one, the others.

The end of the procession was brought up by faces Frank had never seen: a florid uncle; a tousled and insouciant brother; a somnambulistic sister, awake now, and rubbing her eyes; a faithful wife craning her neck to see where her husband had got to; a yellow-raincoated child pushing a bicycle, his cheeks streaked with dirt. The boy broke away from the others and came up to Frank; he leaned forward, his face a pale mask, and whispered, —Have you got your money ready?

Comio shook Frank's shoulder.

—What?

—It's happening.

He led Frank after the procession, which wound toward the edge of the cellar. Those ahead of Frank—detectives and transients he didn't recognize, thin and unsteady on their feet, as though they hadn't eaten in days—spoke in hushed voices of how they had never expected this day to come. Orestes fell in with Frank and Comio, cackling that the gambler would at last get a lesson about the importance of stories.

—And you're going to make us rich, Comio said. Isn't that right, Frank?

The procession climbed a short flight of stairs and stumbled into the light. They stood on a vast and empty stage. To one side, row upon row of empty seats receded to the almost invisible far wall. A pair of masks hung over the stage: one of them stared down, expressionless; the other was expressionless but with its eyes closed. This was the prison theater, where traveling companies sometimes entertained the inmates. They must, Frank thought, have been in the theater's cellar all along.

The air smelled of smoke. Somewhere outside, men were shouting.

—Hey! Over here! the transients called. —The exit's over here.

—Wait up, Frank, said Comio. Don't you remember our bet? The ocean's going to flood the prison.

—Shouldn't we go outside, then?

—Outside? Comio laughed. There's no place safer than where we are right now. You just wait here with us.

Comio winked at Orestes.

Frank wanted to go with the others—wasn't Prudence at the head of the procession? But Comio told him that anyone who went outside was a fool, given what was coming. —The place to be, he said, is high up.

Comio led them across the stage, into a warren of costume racks, spooled cables, spotlights borrowed from the watchtowers and equipped with colored gels, pots of face paint in white and blue, mirrors, rolls of canvas painted to look like the cloudless sky by day, and other rolls painted to look like the sky at night. They climbed catwalks to the balconies from which light and sound were regulated, then ladders to other, narrower balconies from which flats and scrims were hung; metal rungs in the wall led them to the ledges appointed, Comio whispered, for the flying machines, the rain machines with their thick hoses and potbellied cloud generators; the lighting bolts and chariots of papier-mâché which traveled on almost invisible tracks across the sky. Higher still, under the roof of the theater, dangled a host of celestial bodies in paste and cardboard. Comio demonstrated how, by the use of pulleys, any hour or season could be represented; he pointed to the horned moon, the gibbous moon, and the ingenious mechanism for simulating comets and eclipses. Then they emerged onto the roof, where it was raining. The prison lay far below them; the electric fence sparked and crackled, and beyond that rose the prison's many walls, then a great orange light: the city. In the other direction was the harbor, the shore, the limitless darkness of the ocean's embrace.

Something was wrong within the prison. Guards and inmates chased one another in and out of the cell blocks. Some had rifles, and others clubs. The refectory was burning, and the library doors were off their hinges.

—What's going on? Frank asked.

—Panic, said Orestes.

—Why? I thought they didn't know what was going to happen.

—You ask too many questions, Comio said.

—But . . .

—The guards want the prisoners to go to bed, but the prisoners aren't tired, all right? Now be quiet and watch.

—Shouldn't we go down and tell them?

—It's too late, Orestes said.

There was a flash of light from the center of the prison: a plume of sparks rose from the shed that housed the generators, and all the lights in the courtyard went out. For a moment, the prison was returned to the usual cycle of day and night, and seemed to shrink a little. The dark ridges of nearby hills became visible, and the fires on the hills, where, it was rumored, the criminally insane wandered, committing vicious acts in the hope that they would be admitted to the prison and the ministrations of the guards. For a moment the three imagined themselves returning to the city, chilled and miserable but almost free. The boy shook his fist in the air. Then blue emergency lamps came on, shining like marshlights in the puddles that by now extended from one cell block to the next.

—I'm going to warn them, Frank said.

—They won't believe you, said Orestes.

—Wait! said Comio.

Frank turned to go downstairs. Something struck his head, and he fell. When he opened his eyes, he was lying on his back. The sky was entirely dark; it seemed closer than it had before.

—It's happening, Comio said. Look.

Above them loomed the moon. It was larger than Frank had ever seen it, larger than anything; it occluded half the sky. It was as though, for the first time, the true size of a celestial object had been revealed; an astronomical scale had preempted all human distances. The moon was its own map: all its craters and seas were visible, although too bright to look at, for the moon was full. It lit the water and the prison more brightly than they had ever before been lit, revealing everything that was there and many things that were not. Shadows like faces skimmed the uneven surface of the water, reminding Frank of silhouettes he had seen in the trees at the side of the road, walking home from a country dance long ago. The shadows of old buildings appeared, and the shadows of streets Frank had walked once but despaired of finding again. He understood what must happen now that the moon had showed itself. It was only a minute, or two, or ten seconds or less, until the wave appeared on the horizon. It *was* the horizon; the earth had grown tired of being spherical, and re-formed itself as an ellipse, then as a teardrop whose tail approached them with a hiss across the ocean. Less a wave than a wall, less a wall than a long, flat mountain, it shone in the moonlight, the same color as the moonlight; soon it hid the bottom of the moon. On the crest, ships, all the ships of the ocean, bobbed and collapsed, their nets and lines fluttering behind them in the wind. The foot of the wave reached the shore. The buildings beyond the prison's edge vanished in an instant, as did the harbor; the water raced to the foot of the prison wall. Then the wave stooped; it sank, and curled, and sheared the theater's roof from its supports. Frank clung to the roof; it was like flying or being shot from a cannon. For a second, before the wave broke, he could see the ocean floor. It was nothing more than an expanse of dirt and pools of water, coral and silt, sandbars and oyster beds, littered with the mangled bodies of fish and dolphins and whales and old wrecks lost at sea half a hundred years ago, their sides spilling over now with bullion and kelp; skeletons with weights chained to their feet, iron chests and chests of rotten wood, the tarnished helmets of a dozen deep-sea divers lost in a storm; the worn, barnacled stone of lost cities built on sinking islands, whales by the pod, octopi and krakens and larger, wormlike things with polyps and suckers and spines, dredged up from rifts not yet charted by the oceanographers. The wave, advancing, laid bare the foundations of the city: a tangle of cellars and sewers and the secret underground railway that carried officials to and fro in the event of an emergency, the pneumatic tubes that routed urgent messages from one post office to the next; the entrances to mine shafts dug long ago and forgotten now by all but smugglers and troglodytes, gas mains and cisterns and the old graveyard, exhumed, where the skeletons of those who built the city and those who first burned it down, those who laid siege to it and those who sacked it and those who defended the cathedral, the protagonists of a thousand histories and as many lying accounts, shone cleanly in the moonlight. For a moment Frank saw everything at once; then the wave broke, and he fell with it into the boiling city.

THE ENUMERATION OF PARTS

—WE BROUGHT YOU ONE, SOMEONE SAID, and deposited Frank on a cot. He looked unlikely to live much longer. His skin was white as sea foam, and as wet; he shook so violently that the attending doctor could barely slip a needle into his arm. In a moment Frank was still, but so hot that the mercury rose past the last marking in the thermometer, which meant, the doctor observed, that he'd bet Frank was a goner; then he shrugged professionally and set a cool compress over Frank's eyes. For days Frank was fever's candle: he burned, spluttered, flickered, and, he heard afterwards, almost went out altogether. It was a miracle he'd lived, the nuns told him, and they confided that when his fever broke the doctor cursed and threw his stethoscope on the floor; he'd given long odds that their patient would not survive. This, at least, is what the nuns told him later; he knew nothing himself of how he'd come to their hospital.

Faces danced in his fever: there was Prudence, and there Comio, and other,

older faces. His father, who looked in memory not unlike
Orestes, leaned on the wheel of his white car, which had stopped,
for some reason, in the middle of a wheatfield. *It's his heart*, said
Frank's mother, who looked as she had in the photograph, only
darker, and gently lined by the sun. *Do you understand?* A telescope lolled in the back seat, its legs folded like a sleeping child's.
The car shone with reflected suns. Its tracks curved out of sight
behind it, and reappeared ahead only a few feet to the side. *Look
at that*, Frank's mother said. *He must have gone in circles all
night.* Frank opened his eyes. The only people he could see were
nuns, scurrying about in their blue habits with starch-winged
caps. They were very beautiful nuns, he thought, and went back
to sleep. The next day, when he woke up again, he was groggily
conscious of being in the hospital. The day after, his seventh
there, he remembered that something had happened to him, and
on the eighth he remembered what it was. He rang for one of the
nuns. —You haven't seen Comio? Or an old man? His name is
Orestes. They were prisoners, too.

—Of course they were, the nun said.

She put her hand on his forehead.

—But the tidal wave set us free, said Frank.

—Try to sleep, the nun advised. She gave him a cup of wine-red
tonic, and closed the curtains around his bed.

The nuns refused to speak of the prison. Whenever he mentioned the guards, the perpetual light, the years he'd spent in the
laundry, the astronomy and anatomy lessons, they smoothed his
hair and murmured, Hush, as they would to a child. When Frank
asked where he had come from, then, the nuns told him that an
old man and a boy, dead drunk, had brought him in, and that

judging from his smell the nuns had assumed he was of their company. Because Frank was without wallet or papers, the drunks brought him to the nuns' hospital, which was ordinarily for foundlings but had, in these difficult times, assumed responsibility for those unidentified adults who appeared like babies in odd corners of the world. —But the tidal wave? Frank asked. —The revolution, you mean? It's been a hard time for us all, although I wouldn't go to such lengths as you to forget about it.

After that, Frank asked no more questions about how he'd been set free. Months later, however, his sleep would be plagued by dreams in which he stood on a stage, up to his knees in a bucket of salt water, while Orestes blew in his face and Comio, high above the stage, operated the machines which flashed like lightning, rumbled like drums, and dribbled rain onto his fevered face. Frank struggled to climb out of the tub, stumbled, fell in, and got up again. Comio and Orestes roared with laughter. The more Frank tried to get out, the harder they laughed; Orestes, doubled over, rewarded Frank's efforts with a squirt of salt water in the eyes. The dream always ended the same way: Frank said, *I gave it all to the guards,* and Orestes, furious, struck his head with a pail.

Each time he woke from that dream, Frank's legs felt as sore as if he had been running, and it was a long time before he could sleep again.

Frank questioned the nuns about their faith. It was a stern religion, which taught that there was no such thing as individual sin, only communal wrongdoing, for which only institutions could atone. Their religion had nothing but contempt for the hermit and the anchorite; all of its adherents worked in the hospital, or

in the cathedral, or in the school nearby. God does not hear individual prayer, the nuns told him, and changed the compress on
his forehead. Why not? Frank asked. Because, they explained,
God is very far away. Only the loudest prayers reach his ears.
Frank offered to convert to their religion out of gratitude, but was
informed that individual conversions were frowned upon; God
was satisfied only by mass professions of faith. He offered instead
to draw them little portraits of themselves, for keepsakes. When
they brought him a pencil and paper, though, Frank found the
contours that his hand produced so ugly and artless that he erased
them at once, began again, erased again, and gave up. He returned
the paper to the nuns, who understood.

The next day they let him go. The nuns offered him a new suit
of clothes, as was customary: ugly trousers and a cheap cotton
shirt, a wool coat and a knit cap; none of them fit. They pushed a
little money into his hand when they said goodbye at the door of
the hospital. The nuns admitted that they wouldn't pray for him,
because such things weren't allowed, but they wished him good
luck all the same.

The glorious day Bonnie's salon hoped for, Frank gathered
from the newspapers, had come at last. It had been more than a
day, actually, but less than a month, recently ended and already
dwindling in the papers' memories and in the size of the head-
lines' type. Apparently, the buildings to be built and torn down
which Max had spoken of were largely metaphorical. The revolution had changed the city, but only a little: a spit of land at one end
of the harbor was razed, as were the puppeteers' cemetery and the
houseboats where, formerly, independent-minded old people

had festooned the ends of their lives with grand sunsets over the western ocean. The textile museum had been torched, and the Old Library with its thousands of manuscripts. If Justice had come to the city, it was largely in the form of changes to the roster of the municipal employees. The police had mostly been replaced—which meant, Frank hoped, that he would not be arrested again—and a new Mayor presided in City Hall. The Isinglass Museum had a new director, and Lastrade, of the Quadrilateral University, emeritus, had been named Minister of Education. His black-and-white likeness glared happily from the newspaper, over an article about a new program which would teach children to do as their teachers did, not as they said.

These reforms aside, the citizens got on with their lives almost as soon as they had cleaned up the debris which carpeted the streets: slashed portraits and burnt bolts of cloth, cracked urns and burnt spars, and, here and there, one of the blue uniforms which were all that remained of the old prison, where much of the fighting had taken place. This debris was burned in Cathedral Square one evening, to the accompaniment of fireworks and somber music, which livened as the bonfire burned down, until, by morning, the ashes and tired dancers might have been mistaken for the remains of a wedding party. The winter was a busy one for the cafés and movie theaters, the nightclubs and taverns. By the time Frank was released, the buses were running again, though not in such great numbers as before. He thought briefly of going to look for Max, who had apparently become some sort of grand functionary, but decided it would only remind him of Prudence, and besides, how could he show himself in a grand functionary's office, looking as he did? Instead, Frank stumbled to the center of the Cathedral Square and took the first bus to Bellaway's.

The boardinghouse had flourished under the new regime. It had plate-glass doors with BELLAWAY'S written in discreet capitals, and picture windows in the ground-floor parlors; the front of the building had been cleaned so that the stone was white again. Frank rang the bell, and a mustachioed clerk answered. He asked to see James, and, when the clerk told him that no one by that name worked there, asked for Mrs. Bellaway. After a quarter of an hour she came downstairs, splendid in a black satin widow's gown which reached to her ankles, a black ribbon around her neck, and a velvet shawl with jet trim. Underneath the finery, however, she was still very much her long-jawed, square-headed, drab self.

—I can't give you your job back, she said. It's been filled, and besides, you left without giving notice.

—It's all right. I'd rather not work in a laundry again.

—Oh! Mrs. Bellaway seemed relieved. That's all right, then. Will you stay for some tea?

The clerk brought them a pot of weak tea in the back parlor. Mrs. Bellaway told Frank the story of her successes: how the judges, who spent nearly half the year in the city now, had been coming in greater and greater numbers to her establishment; how they had come last spring for the annual convention of judges, and stayed here, and how they were due to come again this spring, and how punctually they paid. —Nothing like a judge when it comes to respecting a woman's finances! Mrs. Bellaway exclaimed. —But where have you been, Frank? I thought you were traveling.

—That's right.

—Oh, how simply wonderful. I've always wanted to travel, but you know how it is when one has obligations.

A bell rang at Mrs. Bellaway's side.

—Did you see lots of things?

—All the wonders of the world, Frank said.

—Well, that's very nice.

—I was wondering if you know where James is? Frank asked.

—Who? Oh, your friend. I have no idea. He ran off years ago.

—He didn't leave an address?

The bell rang again. Mrs. Bellaway shook her head and rose to her wide, slippered feet. —And now if you'll excuse me. Business! It never ends, you know, it simply never ends . . .

She left Frank to find his own way out. He looked for James in the phone book at the front desk, but his friend wasn't listed.

Frank rode the buses without design for an hour or two, and found himself in a foggy neighborhood where the sagging sky was propped up on the sharp tops of telephone poles. With the money the nuns gave him, he took a room in a cheap hotel behind the bus depot, a yard with a chain-link fence which reminded him faintly of the prison. Empty buses roared past, beginning and ending their circular journeys. Their headlights lit the room a brilliant yellow five or six times an hour. Frank couldn't sleep; he sat all night in a chair facing the window, watching the buses and, beyond their yard, an illuminated sign which belonged to the doll factory. The sign was a rosy-cheeked girl's head, fifteen feet across, mounted on top of the building and lit at night from just below its chin, which gave the smiling face a diabolical expression.

The next morning, as soon as the factory was open, Frank went to see the manager. He waited for an hour outside the office; then the manager's assistant led him in. The office had a large window overlooking the inside of the factory and all the assembly line, from the distant corner where the armatures were put together, the bins of limbs and torsos and heads, to the tables where the dolls were painted, the tables where they were dressed, and the pallets on which the assembled dolls were stored before being shipped out. Something about the finished dolls caught Frank's eye, but before he could decide what it was, the manager's assistant pulled him away from the window and led him toward the far end of the room.

The manager's face was knobbed and wrinkled as though it had been pickled. He sat behind a small desk, buried in invoices and shipping bills, catalogues and procedure manuals, with his feet on the only other chair in the room. —What is it, he asked curtly.

—I'm looking for a job, Frank said.

—A job. The manager tugged his lower lip and let it snap back into place. —Do you have any skills?

—I know a little astronomy. Some anatomy. And I can wash clothes.

—Dolls don't get dirty.

—I'm a hard worker.

The manager wrote something on a form. When he was done, he licked his pencil's eraser with satisfaction.

—I used to paint, said Frank. My work's in the Isinglass Museum. That is, I think it's still there.

The manager looked up.

—They called me Hugo, Frank said. I mean, that's not my

name, but it's what they called me. I was the great artist of the missing. I painted pictures . . .

—Sure you did. The manager laughed. We're all artists, here. Of one kind or another.

—Then I won't take up any more of your time . . .

—Wait. The manager waved for Frank to remain. —The pay's bad and the hours are long. Working conditions are a disgrace. We have to bribe the Labor Department to keep from being closed down.

—I don't mind.

—Then you can start right away. Joseph! The assistant came back, holding a clipboard. —Get this Hugo . . .

—It's Frank.

—Get this Frank to work on eyelids. He glared at Frank. —Botch three dolls and you're fired.

Joseph showed him to a bench near the middle of the line. This was where the dolls' heads were assembled. Workers threaded artificial hair through the holes in their skulls, snapped glass eyes into their sockets, and secured movable eyelids on tiny tracks below the eyebrows. Joseph showed him in a perfunctory way how the eyelids were installed: bend the lid, slip it onto the track, like this, and let it snap back. Always jiggle the lid to see that it works. Then pass the head on to the hair people. Payday's Friday, no advances. Good luck! He left Frank with a bin of lifelike plastic eyelids and a steadily growing pile of lidless, hairless doll heads. These were, Frank saw, no ordinary dolls. They were almost as large as people, and almost as carefully made; their features were individualized to the point that there were hundreds, perhaps thousands, of distinct doll faces and doll bodies. Some of them could speak, thanks to a clever mechanical apparatus placed in their chests farther down the line; others could comb their hair, dance, or clap. They were the fantastic, almost-living dolls that Frank had seen in store windows in the rich parts of town, dressed in human clothes, sitting in perfect repose in authentic replicas of rooms.

Frank set to work giving them eyelids. The work wasn't hard, once he got the hang of it; the trick was not to be distracted by the face or the color of the eyes—some of them were beautiful shades of gray and hazel, and others interestingly yellowed and blood-shot—but to concentrate on the steps: bend, slide, snap, jiggle, pass, and repeat. Frank began slowly, and the hair people called to him more than once to hurry up, but by the end of the day he had almost finished his quota. It was true that in order to do this he had to stay until midnight, but it wasn't far from the factory to an all-night cafeteria, and from there to the hotel, and he slept soundly until the next morning.

The work got easier up to a point, then became monotonous. At the end of a week Frank kept up with the eye man; after two weeks he had perfected his technique, and it was the hair people's turn to complain that he was making them look bad. When the installation of eyelids became purely mechanical, Frank noticed the dolls' faces again. He imagined that they were the faces of acquaintances, and tried to infer their character from the cast of their plastic: this one was spiteful, he decided, and that one not to be trusted with money; one would sing beautifully when drunk, and another would never live up to his own expectations.

One day the eye man passed him a head whose character he knew already: it was Prudence's. Frank frowned, blinked, and

held the face to the light. When he turned it one way, it looked just like the photographer of the dead, and when he turned it the other, less so. In any case, the resemblance was not exact since the head was as yet hairless, and the lips and brows hadn't been painted in. Frank examined the head until the hair people grumbled; then he gave it lids and passed it along. The hair they threaded through the skull was the color of Prudence's hair. Frank had to hurry to catch up with the eye man's work; he was busy until the end of the day, when he went back to the manager's office.

—No advances, the manager said. Didn't Joseph tell you?

—It's not for that. I want to look at a catalogue.

—What for? You can't afford one of these dolls. Trust me.

—I might save up.

The manager sighed. —Well, you can dream.

The catalogue was as thick as a long novel, and all on glossy paper. Frank skimmed through it until he found the doll with Prudence's face. It was dressed in a pink-and-yellow jumpsuit and skis, and straddled a mound of artificial snow. Alpine Monique was the doll's name. It cost more than Frank would make in a year—but came with its own ski bag, dark glasses, and a bottle of imitation schnapps. Frank would have bet that it was Prudence underneath the costume, although the doll's profile was slightly sharper, and its lips had a cast that Prudence's lips, in Frank's experience at least, had never assumed. Might Prudence have modeled for a doll company, long ago? She hadn't mentioned it. But it was the sort of thing that one might not boast about, to have a thousand Alpine Monique dolls made in one's likeness.

In his room Frank tried to remember Prudence, and whether among the stories she told him there had been any mention of dolls.

Weeks passed. The city was immersed in the sort of winter rain which leaves the air wet until the next downpour and makes the citizens short-tempered. Whether it was because he'd caught their grumpiness, or for some other reason, one day Frank let the head he was working on—a blank, smiling masculine head—fly out of his hands; it bounced off a table and landed on the floor, cracked beyond repair. It was the first time he had broken a head.

—What do I do? he asked the eye man.

—Take it to Damaged Parts. The eye man pointed to a door at the far side of the factory. Carrying the head under his arm, Frank walked to the Damaged Parts repository, a long room lined with bins full of cracked and warped and burned limbs, mispainted heads and miscast torsos, unstrung armatures and double-jointed hands. The clerk in attendance, a young woman in gray overalls, was busy counting broken arms.

—Excuse me? Frank coughed. —I've got a head.

She turned from her inventory.

—Evelyn?

Her hair was shorter than it had been, and her face thinner. Glasses had cured her squint; they magnified her eyes, so that she seemed to watch everything with exaggerated surprise.

—Frank! It is Frank, isn't it? What are you doing here?

—I've broken a head, Frank said dumbly.

—Here. She wrote her telephone number on the corner of a piece of paper, ripped it off, and handed it to Frank. —Call me this evening. There's so much I want to tell you . . . Are you still making those pictures? No time to talk now. But this evening, all right?

She recorded the broken head and Frank's name, and went back to the arms.

They met in a cavernous, dim café frequented mostly by bus drivers. In a back booth, out of range of their talk of schedules and accidents, Evelyn explained that life with Carolyn and her father had become intolerable after Rosalyn left: Charles was always comparing the two girls who remained to their missing sister, who had become his favorite, now that she was gone. Besides, Carolyn's husband the plumber was a boor. Evelyn had heard, since, that he'd drowned because of a miscalculation of the Coriolis effect. She couldn't say that she was sorry. From Rosalyn and James she'd heard nothing; she didn't even know that they had come back to the city. Evelyn ran away, and lived for years in a lighthouse on the northern coast, at the end of a rocky promontory where the current ran so strong, the sailors said, that even to see the lighthouse's beacon meant you would run aground. She tended the light and counted the ships that passed— ghost ships, mostly, for the shipping lanes had shifted long ago to less dangerous waters—and did what she could to pull mariners from the surf when their ships broke up. In her spare time she drew seascapes and taught herself double-entry accounting, the better to log the passing wrecks. When the lighthouse was closed down by the Ministry of Trade, which had decided on the basis of her reports that the beacon did more harm than good, Evelyn came back to the city, her head full of travelers' tales, equations, and tide charts.

The revolution came soon after, and because of the mistrust of educated people which it brought in, Evelyn couldn't find work anywhere but at the doll factory. (Did you tell the manager you were an artist? Frank asked. —Yes, how did you guess?) Because she knew accounting, they gave her the job in Damaged Parts, which was easier than making dolls, and paid better besides, so that Evelyn could afford a two-room apartment on the far side of the bus depot, where the spluttering of engines reminded her a little of the sea.

They met the following night in Evelyn's room. It had been rented to her by a mother whose son, a railway engineer, had been missing ever since the construction of a distant tunnel. Boxes of his clothes and childhood paraphernalia filled the closet, unopened despite the landlady's having invited Evelyn to rummage around and take anything she could use. Aside from the boxes, the room came with a hot plate, a divan, and a window which let in the perfect amount of light in the morning. Evelyn had decorated the walls with her paintings, gray-and-blue canvases of the sea in different weathers. Gulls dotted the sky, and rocks the shore; between the gulls and the rocks, color faded into color, creating the impression of distance in which a ship might suddenly appear, founder, and be lost.

—But what have you been up to, Frank? Evelyn asked.

Frank began to tell her what had happened, then stopped. Prison had broken his life into parts, and the parts were still ajumble; to put them in order would have been the work of months, if not longer. Because he had to say something, he improvised a past. He had left Mrs. Bellaway's, he said, to try his hand at the law, clerking at night for a firm that specialized in automobile accidents. His job was to wander the streets, looking for wrecks to represent. He learned little about the law and much about traffic, Frank explained, uneasy and delighted that he could invent a life for himself with so little effort. For instance, in Cathedral Square, accidents happened chiefly in the early hours of the morning, when the pattern of red and green lights changed to allow the nuns to process to matins uninterrupted; the highways that bordered the river were rich in suicides, as more citizens than was generally suspected wanted, in their final moments, to have the choice between drowning and being crushed. Frank's career in the law had ended one night with a premonition. He wandered through the part of the city where the buildings were made of iron, until he became certain that a collision of litigious proportions would happen in a gardened square nearby. He walked until he found the square at the back of a slum by the freight yards. The premonition, however, had come too soon: Frank saw the headlights of the schoolbus coming from one direction, and from the other heard the oil tanker's horn. Here he made his mistake. He stepped into the street, waving at one vehicle and the other, shouting, Stop! Stop! The truck veered into the garden and the schoolbus half-climbed the sidewalk, avoiding collision with the tanker, but not with Frank. He had spent months in the hospital, he said, and when he got out, the law, which had no use for prescience, would have nothing to do with him.

—It must haunt you, Evelyn said.

—Not really. I don't think I had a future in the law anyway.

—Did you ever think of taking up drawing? I mean seriously? Because I remember . . .

—Do you know? I don't think it was drawing that interested me. Really.

—Oh?

—It was more the subjects.

—Oh. Evelyn blushed. Well. You know, I'd be happy to pose for you. If you want.

—That's all right.

—But I'd like it.

Frank shrugged. —Did you rescue many mariners?

—Not so many. Ten or fifteen.

—What were they like?

—Nothing special. Like you or me, only more, I don't know, more talkative. I suppose because they'd spent so much time cooped up. They were awfully glad to see me. Because I saved them, of course there's that, but also because of the novelty. Hard to know what you'd do, on a ship, waiting, always. Apparently they told each other stories.

—Tell me one.

Evelyn sat beside Frank on the divan, so close that her knee touched his knee. Her story wandered like a ghost ship from port to port: now it was about a sea captain who traded with the moon, which, in those days, docked on certain nights in earthly harbors; and now it was about the captain's bride, an intelligent but melancholy woman, who waited for her beloved in a seaside house where she gardened, and spent long hours on the balcony, sighing at the horizon. The moon caught a plague from the people of the earth, and the captain was sent off to find the only cure for their disease, a plant called lady's-tears, which, had the captain only known it, grew in abundance in his bride's garden, watered by her tears and those, colder but no less salty, of the ocean. But the sea captain, who had no eye for plants, sailed off in the opposite direction and . . . Evelyn shook her head. —I don't remember the rest, she said. —If only I'd been a sailor! They tell stories as if it were the most natural thing in the world.

By this time Frank and Evelyn had sunk toward each other on the divan, so that Evelyn's right hip pressed against Frank's left thigh and his left hand lay atop her right leg.

—So much happens in our lives, doesn't it? she said. I mean, we do one thing and then we do another and by the time we come back to the first thing it's something entirely different, do you know what I mean?

—Hm.

—And I wonder if it would have been different if you had drawn me when we first met, and maybe you would have found a talent for it, and I would have been your first model, and I wouldn't have left for the coast and you wouldn't have gone to work for Mrs. Bellaway, and then we'd be famous together and we wouldn't be working in the doll factory, although maybe not, because I might not have been a terribly good model, and in any case I have my own work, and who knows.

As she spoke, Evelyn leaned closer and closer, until Frank could not help but kiss her. Her tongue wriggled as though it were still trying to speak. Evelyn rested her hands on Frank's back; her breasts pressed against his breast. Their legs turned one way and another on the narrow sofa to make room for the conjunction of their upper halves. Frank closed his eyes and opened them again; Evelyn opened hers and closed them just as Frank opened his eyes for the second time, and so it went, each of them closing his or her eyes just as the other's opened, as though they could bear neither to look at each other nor to let the kiss pass unobserved. The more he looked, however, the more Frank became aware of the stuffing and springs in the divan, the seascapes behind Evelyn's head, the window and the shelf of blue crockery. Part of him hoped that at some moment, by embracing Evelyn in the right way, he might make the room disappear. His secret ambition in kissing her was to cause the world to vanish as it had once vanished for James and Rosalyn on their walks together; it would not occur to him until much later that he had gone about it in the wrong way.

On Sundays the doll factory was closed; it was the workers' one day off. If Frank and Evelyn were not sitting on the divan in Evelyn's room, watching the light change as the sun set behind the depot, then they wandered one of the city's many gardens, choosing new paths through the labyrinths, admiring the gazebos on hills here and there, and the topiary in the shape of fleeing lovers. Each morning, one would call the other to exchange dreams; at night, exhausted by the doll factory, they told stories of when they had been children. They included each other in the telling as though they had grown up together. It was then that Frank began to remember his first childhood, before he went to live with James. Scenes he'd thought lost for good drifted once again into his mind. He told Evelyn about birthday parties (which she must have missed on account of illness), and trips to provincial towns which she might have taken if Frank's parents had room for another child in the car. He remembered other things, too: how his mother had a workshop in which she studied the animals and plants of her southern province, and the books with sepia diagrams which told her what the parts of every living thing were called. He remembered the radio burbling at night, water splashing in the sink as she washed dishes, the smell of wood smoke, the turtle which had appeared on their porch one afternoon, miraculously, a refugee from who knew what body of water. What had become of it? Frank didn't remember. He said nothing to Evelyn about the turtle, the fire, the dishes, the radio, as she could not have participated, even hypothetically, in their perception.

Soon they felt that they had known each other quite well long ago. They wondered together what had become of the friends who had built themselves a raft, and what happened to the maid who, until she was dismissed, used to rap their heads with the butt end of a pair of scissors to check that their skulls had not become hollow. They divided the labor of cooking and washing up, dusting the pictures and scrubbing the floor with a worn brown sponge, washing the windows and putting out fresh traps for the insects.

On Evelyn's birthday Charles invited them to come around, take a drink, and sit with him for an hour or two in his muddy yard. Immobility had ruined the hunchback's memory, as though he could only fix things in his mind by seeing them and hurrying away. He confused Carolyn and Evelyn, Evelyn and Rosalyn, Rosalyn and Carolyn, Glenda and Rosalyn, Frank and James and the drowned plumber. He butchered a small cake and asked Frank to tell him please what it was he did for a living. —I want grandchildren! he roared as Carolyn took the dishes into the house. —Don't come back until you've brought me my posterity! My posterity! Frank and Evelyn repeated the phrase as a joke for weeks afterwards.

Aside from this ruin of a man in a distant part of the city and the occasional Alpine Monique head, there was little to remind Frank of the other life which had interposed itself between the mysterious comforts of his childhood and the easy regularity of his days with Evelyn. Only once, as he crossed the Cathedral Square on the way home from the open-air market, a woman called his name. The square squawked and thrummed with its usual complement of musicians, mimes, acrobats, caricaturists, spectacular cripples, and stern storytellers who exacted coins from their audience at each suspenseful moment. Frank, struggling to balance a bag of dates, a bundle of kindling, and a sack of long soup bones, at first didn't hear the call, then ignored it; but the woman would not be put off. She grabbed at his arm.

—Frank! Oh! Frank!

The bones slipped from their sack; Frank cursed and turned around.

—I'm sorry. I didn't mean to . . . The woman let go Frank's arm and stared with remorse at her hands.

—Rosalyn?

She looked as though she belonged in the square: her frayed coat and tangled hair spoke of days spent in the absence of mirrors. At her side stood an equally ragged girl of five or six, who watched Frank to see what he would drop next. As she picked up the bones, Rosalyn began one sentence after another: —So you're alive! It's so strange . . . They said you weren't, at the prison . . .

—This is Isabel. Isabel, say hello to our old friend Frank, the famous artist.

—I'm going to be an engineer, Isabel said.

—Yes, aren't you? And James is here, we're just on our way to get James. He plays guitar these days. But where are you living? Do you still draw those pictures? He'll be so happy to see you. Do you want to come with us? For dinner? I can't promise you much, but maybe with a few of these bones . . . But you have to come, Frank, come and tell us everything.

—I can't. Not now. I'm expected home. Frank was seized by a guilty panic, as though something were being demanded of him, something he had borrowed, and lost, and could neither replace nor explain.—Another time.

—Oh, of course I understand. Rosalyn wrote out her address and gave it to Frank. —It's not so far away if you don't mind walking uphill. You'll come, won't you? Maybe you could give James some advice. He's an artist now, and he admires you so much, Frank, and your drawings—

—I'll come.

—I'm building a ship, Isabel said. All by myself.

Frank gathered the bones in his arms, and wondered for a moment what it would be like to hold a child. Then he had taken a step, and another. Rosalyn and Isabel disappeared behind a crowd of mimes separated from one another by their small, invisible rooms.

To celebrate their engagement Frank bought Evelyn a puppet, a sailor with a wooden head and a body of bright blue cloth, hands of pink felt, and a miniature pipe and sextant.

—To tell me stories with, Frank said, and Evelyn smiled.

—To tell *you* stories?

—Well, for now.

In return she gave him a stack of brochures. —I've been saving, she said. Look! She spread them out on the bed, and unfolded them one by one. They bore photographs of a part of the city reclaimed from the bay, where houses on small plots were being made available to enterprising young couples with nothing against a little ocean mist.

ALL THE SAME, FRANK DEVELOPED CERTAIN beliefs about the dolls. The more he looked at Alpine Monique, the more he was convinced that the doll's head was nothing more than one of his sketches fleshed out in three dimensions, or an aggregate of several sketches, full-face portraits and three-quarter profiles. He told himself that it was only a coincidence. After all, just as there were only seven hundred and eighty-three dolls in the most recent catalogue, so there could be only so many types of human face. In a city as large as this one, it stood to reason that some of them would repeat. Frank remembered times when he had nearly touched some young mother on the elbow and said, Prudence? But the resemblance only went so far. Before he could put out his hand, the woman turned, tugging her child away. The cast of her face was her own, not Prudence's, and her way of inclining her head, and the impatience in her voice—Frank blushed, let his hand fall, and hurried on. Even if Monique was Prudence, the coincidence was only unsettling.

There was no reason why the doll factory couldn't have gotten hold of one or two of Frank's sketches; they had been widely distributed, and indeed several might still hang in the Isinglass Museum. What troubled Frank was the possibility that the sketches' transformation into bodies, albeit artificial ones, might be due to something more mysterious than the lathe, the vat, the extruder, and the injection mold. Each Monique might have a bit of Prudence in it, some tiny fraction of the photographer's life that, like a starfish, might be grown back into the entire person. As the Monique doll was not a popular model, he was by and large able to put this unwelcome belief out of his mind. Each time Monique's lidless eyes arrived on his table, however, Frank found himself thinking, What if it's her? What if it's her? It's *not* her, he told himself. It helped to say it aloud; fortunately, the factory floor was noisy enough that no one heard him.

Frank and Evelyn arranged to visit the site of a new development, with an eye to making a down payment if they found something cheap enough and adequately sheltered from the wind. On Saturday morning Evelyn opened the brochure and pointed to the designs that appealed to her the most: a narrow white house with shutters of green wood; a round house of brick with a round bedroom upstairs, ringed by windows. —And think, Frank! We'll have an extra room for me to paint in, and you to read or do what you like. Although perhaps we'll use it for something else? In any case, we can do whatever we want, if we own it. Which do you like better, wood or brick?

Frank went to work without having answered the question. He thought about it as he snapped eyelids into their tracks, jiggled, and began again. Wood or brick? It hardly mattered. Frank saw that he was working on another Prudence, that is, another Monique. —It's *not* her, he said. He passed her head to the hair people, and watched them thread black fibers through the skull, tie them off just under the scalp, part and brush the hair. In fact, it didn't matter much where he lived. Although he would prefer not to be so close to the water, because of all the things it reminded him of. Although there was the spare room, yes, it would be good to have that, and perhaps in time the house would fill with children, who would make proper use of the yard, the attic and the basement, and the communal playground, ornamented with slides and brightly colored concrete animals, which figured prominently in the brochure. That was where he was heading: toward a life of real children and imitation animals. The heads piled up at Frank's table. In time the children would leave for careers in distant parts of the city. Frank and Evelyn would retire; perhaps one of them would take up carpentry, and the spare room would be made over into a shop, where they would make keepsakes to give the children and neighbors. Frank followed these thoughts all afternoon, planning his retirement, decrepitude, and eventual death. It was strange to think that the rest of his life could be predicted, anticipated, even experienced in advance. Adulthood had a simple order to it, like the assembly of a doll.

Frank had taken too long to finish his work; only the packers and loaders remained in the factory, hoisting dolls from their pallets and settling them in boxes, carrying the boxes to the trucks which waited to deliver the week's production in time for Sunday morning. Frank wandered over to where they worked, and saw for the first time the specially designed cases in which the dolls

were shipped, sturdy wood boxes lined in white cloth. Alpine Monique lay with the rest, her arms folded across her chest, skis by her side and bottle on her hip, awaiting adventure. Without thinking, Frank slid the tongue of the lid into its grooves, picked up the box, and carried it toward the the factory's edge. He passed between two trucks and kept walking into the street, the box under his arm like a bulky instrument case. Frank turned a corner, then another, and found himself in a crowd between two stores, the windows of one full of fish and the windows of the other full of spades, shovels, machines for planting posts in the earth and machines for finding metal underground. Housewives and old gentlemen hurried back and forth across the street, making their last purchases for the weekend. No one seemed to notice Frank or to remark on the box he carried. He walked until a bus stopped beside him; then he got on and asked the driver what the best route was to the beach.

Frank must have got turned around, or the driver left him off at the wrong spot; he stepped out of the bus and found himself on a dirt road between a pine forest and a cliff. The ocean lay below him. He heard the waves sucking at the rocks as the tide retreated; pink and violet men-of-war bobbed listlessly in the tide pools, and streaks of phosphorescent algae lit the water as the sky deepened past indigo into night. Frank shouted after the bus, but it had already taken off; its taillights lurched around a turn and disappeared. Wearily he carried the box along the road, until he found a place where he could climb down toward the water. Although cold, windy, and covered in sharp stones, the beach was not entirely empty: a few stragglers in overcoats marched up and down; others sat with their backs to the giant rocks that dotted the shore, and warmed their hands at fires of flotsam and driftwood; still others climbed the rocks and leaned as far forward as they could, looking out to sea. It was as though the revolution had returned this part of the city to an earlier time, when fewer people trudged up and down the coast. Of course it wouldn't last. Soon the rocks would be worn down here, too, and staircases carved into the cliff; a boardwalk would be built over the tidepools, and the jellyfish would smother in cigarette butts; soon the surf would be drowned out by the sound of a hundred thousand well-soled feet, and everything would be as it had been before. In the interim, Frank enjoyed the wildness of the coast. Whistling to himself, he picked his way among the rocks until he reached the edge of the fens. There he set the doll's box down, and leaned against a boulder. Frank folded his coat and sat on it in the lee of the wind.

He waited until it was entirely dark to open the box. He found the doll's narrow shoulders and her head of porcelain; he pulled her upright and put his arm around her waist; then, feeling her knees give out and her torso slip from his grasp, Frank arranged her so that she sat beside him, and together they watched the moon's slow rise over the ocean. Hardly anyone remained on the beach: only the old pensioners who could do without sleep, a few children who had snuck out to drink and kiss, and one or two beachcombers with shuttered lanterns, collecting the last of the coins dropped during the day. Some time later, when the moon, high above them, cast shadows in the shape of ships over the waves, Frank turned to the doll and whispered, —Prudence?

She said nothing, but he could feel her head turn toward him, and hear the counterweights of her eyelids click.

—Prudence. He sighed. I've missed you terribly. I looked all over the city for you, in the places we used to go and places where you would never have gone of your own free will, because I thought you might have been kidnapped, or worse. I imagined you were being held for ransom, that the kidnappers sent your family notes asking for more money than they could pay, and the notes grew more and more threatening, until one day I imagined that parts of you began to arrive in the mail, at first just tiny parts but then digits, extremities, limbs. Or was it because you owed money? Or did you support someone beyond your means, a lover who wanted an apartment with a view of the water? Or was a child involved? Did you buy her presents which she confessed to losing almost as soon as she accepted them, but you couldn't meet her without a gift in your hands, Prudence, because you had been terribly cold to her when she was just a baby? Did you flee the child, and the debt, to settle in the country, a hermitess in a village of hermits, and did you make a living taking pictures at weddings? Did you move across the river, change your name, dye your hair, buy dark glasses, a cowl, a dog; did you hide among the ladies who support themselves by fishing children's teeth from the sewers and selling them to tourists in the Cathedral Square? Were you in a car accident? Did you lose your memory? Did the family of the man who hit you take you in, and lodge you guiltily; did they teach you to walk again, to speak, to tend their garden and waterwheel? Or did your grandmother fall ill and did you go to tend her, and did she linger? Did you fall victim to an act of terrorism, God knows the city has enough enemies, or to an act of patriotism, God knows it's easy to be mistaken for a foreigner, or to an act of God, a man-made disaster, a degenerative disease? Were you locked away because of a palsy, an ague, tremors, buboes, the signs of an incurable disease for which all they can do is quarantine you and never speak of you again? Just tell me that it wasn't me, that it wasn't something I did.

—I hardly know, the doll said. In general, I don't think about the past.

—What's the last thing you remember?

—Mountains dotted with log houses. I remember hearths and bowls of soups, stiff drinks, paths through the snow, icy hills, the winter sky.

—No, no. Those aren't real memories. You were a photographer.

—The days were very short, and everything turned blue just after sunset.

—You worked for the police department.

—I don't remember.

—You knew a young man.

—I knew several. One was rich, and another sang; a third knew every fold of the mountains.

—He loved you.

—That's not for me to say, the doll said. But I think he loved his mountains more.

—You went out with him at night to take pictures of the dead, don't you remember?

—At night we sat by the fire and he told me how he'd found seashells on the peaks he'd climbed as a child.

—But you know who I am, don't you?

—You gave me eyelids, the doll said, to shut out the world at someone else's whim.

—And before that?

—Before that I had no eyes.

—Then you don't remember anything? Frank sighed and leaned his head against the boulder. The doll was only a doll, and Prudence would not be returned to him, not even for the space of a night. He would bring Monique back to the factory tomorrow, and hope that she had not been missed; he would wish her well and send her off to some child's pretend châlet, to tell stories of elegant lovers in a world Frank could neither afford nor understand.

An old man must have got lost somewhere in the fens. Frank heard his voice grow louder and softer, move closer to the water and then farther away. As it approached, he could make out the words of a song:

> O, *we're old and we're cold and the missing aren't coming,*
> *The missing aren't coming today or tomorrow;*
> *Today or tomorrow our fingers will stiffen,*
> *Our fingers will stiffen, our toes will soon follow;*
> *Our toes will soon follow our hearts to the grave;*
> *Our hearts to the grave have long ago fled,*
> *Have long ago fled when we learned that the missing*
> *The missing are dead and the living are old . . .*

And so on until the voice faded again. After a minute the doll remarked, —You know? That reminds me of a story.

—About the mountains?

—No. Listen.

The Despair Camera

As a girl the photographer had been lonely. She was the youngest daughter of a large family, and her sisters had tired of their rope games and jumping games and counting games long before she was born, so that she was expected even as a small child to entertain herself. She lived in a large house, for the previous generations of her family had been larger still. There were unused wings to this house, and corridors of rooms reserved for no human purpose: one room for the morning light to cross the floor and another for the sunset to sink down the walls, bleaching stripes in the wallpaper. The house had set aside a room for the ravages of mice, and another, high up in the turret, where spiders were encouraged to build their webs; the basement held a suite of cellars and subcellars favorable to the fermentation of wine. The photographer had never found an end to the rooms and corridors. Each time she went walking, she stopped short in the middle of a hall or in a gallery where suits of armor made themselves at home. Suddenly the absence of people struck her and she called out, afraid that something might have happened to her family while she was away. Hearing no voice but her own, she ran back to the populous parts of the house, and for days listened patiently to the perfectly alien concerns of her sisters, aunts, and cousins. For years she was content, if not happy, to explore, be frightened, and return. As she grew older and learned the words for more complicated misfortunes, she began to ask what had happened to those who had once lived in the rest of the house. Her father answered her questions as best he could. The suits of armor belonged to a great-uncle, now deceased, who had taken a special interest in those things that concealed the imperfections of the human form; beyond the first hall stretched a second, full of corsets and glass eyes, and beyond that lay a gallery of false limbs, subtly curved mirrors, and cameras equipped with flattering lenses. A collateral branch of the family had stocked up the wine years ago, before they found that they had a genetic intolerance for mold and moved to a drier climate. The turret had been the province of relations by marriage, poor but distinguished families who used to amuse themselves by running races up and down the stairs at night. Now, as she walked, the photographer imagined all these relatives, dead, emigrated, or exiled, back in their places. The clubfooted uncle sat by the window reading ladies' magazines; the wine collectors sneezed and coughed behind their bins, and the blue-bloods fell shrieking down the carpeted stairs; they borrowed wheelchairs from the uncle, who got drunk on the wine of the collateral branch, who begged to be admitted into the breezy rooms of the blue-bloods. The house took on a certain order. Some days the photographer wondered whether any of the relatives her father described had actually lived there, or whether he was only making up stories to entertain her and to conceal his ignorance; but the fact of it was that the rooms were there and had to be explained somehow.

By the time she left home, the photographer's sisters were married to gamblers, scamps, spendthrift bankers, inventors of glass clocks and perpetual-motion machines. Many had left their husbands or attained an early widowhood, so that they all required their parents' support. The family had no money left for their youngest daughter; they offered her instead a choice of any artifact she liked from the family home. She took one of the great-uncle's cameras, the only heirloom that came with a carrying case. The camera was of a variety not manufactured in the city anymore: a number of filters and colored gels supplemented its lens in such a way as to compensate for the deformations wrought on the subject by despair. With this, the photographer set up shop. Her advertisement was two photographs of herself, one taken with an ordinary camera, and one with her uncle's trick camera; she remarked unhappily on the contrast between the two. Others must have noticed it, too; soon the despairing, or more often their families, telephoned her to schedule appointments, house calls, group portraits, and wedding photographs. She took the Mayor's picture, and the Archbishop's; her photographs graced all the publications of the Quadrilateral University, and there was no end to the luminaries whose pictures she might have taken, were it not for a telephone call which summoned her, late one night, to the house of one of the city's great deforesters. The family wanted a portrait of the heir, pronto, because he had fallen into a funk from which they feared he would not otherwise emerge. She heard a gunshot just as she arrived at the gate. The heir had found one of the pistols hidden in the armoire and shot himself in the heart before it could be hidden somewhere else. He was dead by the time a servant led her into the room. I'm sorry, the photographer said, and turned to go. Unpack your camera, said the deforester. We've already paid for you to come here, haven't we? Take your picture.

The heir was propped up in a chair and a little blood was wiped from the corner of his mouth. The shutter clicked, and the photographer packed her camera away again, happy to be gone from the house. When she developed the film, however, she noticed a strange thing. The filter had cleared the son's face of despair, just as it was supposed to; in fact, his expression and even the attitude of his head had changed completely. He looked up and to one side, toward his father, with a mixture of rage and satisfaction; the deforester looked away with calculated relief. The photographer could hardly stand to look at the prints, but when a servant called a few days later, asking for the negative, she refused to give it up. You'll be well paid for it, the servant said, and when she refused again, the deforester himself came to visit her studio. You understand that the picture might be misunderstood, he told her. It's often hard to understand what goes on in families, from the outside. Still she refused to give him the negative. What do you plan to do with it? he asked. Nothing, she said. It will go badly with you if you keep it, the deforester said, and when she refused again, he left.

Her reputation was ruined almost immediately. Rumors spread that she could erase the effects of despair only by making her subjects look enraged; other rumors implied that her talent sprang from some indignity she had suffered as a child. Customers canceled their orders and warned their friends; the studio emptied out and the telephone was disconnected, by accident, they said, but she couldn't afford to have it reinstalled. Having nothing else to do, she stared day and night at the negative that had ruined her. The heir's expression she understood at once: it spoke of expectations that scaled ever upward, like a wall that grew as you climbed it. She wondered only that he had lived so long. The father's face puzzled her more. What was he looking at? After a week she remembered: the gun, which lay on the floor where the son had dropped it. At once she formed the conviction that the deforester had hidden the gun for the son to find, that her photograph revealed not a suicide but a murder of sorts. She took the negative immediately to the police. The desk sergeant found it intriguing, but admitted that there was nothing he could do in the absence of an investigation, charges, or proof. She left the photograph as evidence against a future crime. A week later the deforester, afraid perhaps of blackmail, or perhaps because the woods that once ringed the city had been turned into pulp, timber, and pencils, left the city, traveling south with a mistress and a new name. While the photographer followed the deforester's flight—his photograph, taken from a little farther away, smiling a little more, appeared each day among the middle folds of the newspaper—the picture she had taken circulated through the various departments of the police force. Forensics was impressed by the wound in the heir's chest, which, when despair was compensated for, revealed either extreme clumsiness or a struggle, perhaps internal, for the possession of the gun. Analysis read into the father's face not only murder but fraud as well, as was in fact discovered when the hardwood supplied by the deforester turned out to be stolen from private copses and botanical gardens. Ballistics thought it saw bullet holes in the far wall. Disguises found a seam at the base of the wife's neck. Buildings and Furniture wondered about the nameless third parties implied by the arrangement of the chairs. For the camera, by means of some secret mirror behind the shutter, or perhaps because of a flaw in the lens, had this property as well: its pictures compensated for the despair of those who saw them, presenting the viewer with a world of renewed suspicion.

When, six months later, the deforester was suspected of having strangled a maid in a city to the south, he was convicted by means of that one picture, which, the witnesses agreed, looked nothing like the deforester, but resembled exactly the man they had seen descending the hotel stairs, balling a stocking between his hands.

By then the photographer was already employed by the police. Her photographs brought far more criminals to justice than had previously been suspected to exist. The murdered cried after their killers; pedestrians slain by motorists or masonry pointed with their crushed arms and unnaturally tilted faces to the negligence that had done them in. Even those who died of natural causes accused someone or other, a landlady who had set the heat too low or an old wife guilty of administering too much medication, or too little. Prosecutors worked double shifts to process all the accused. The prisons filled with new criminals, who by and large had not been aware of their intention to do wrong, and so were particularly difficult to rehabilitate.

At first the citizens celebrated each conviction; then, as more and more of them were arrested, they grew silent and watched their actions carefully. They abandoned the dying and the accident-prone, the infirm and the deranged and those in hazardous occupations, so that the dead might not accuse them. Mourners no longer visited the graveyard; relatives stopped calling one another, for fear that they might hear news of an incriminating death. A true despair set in, unlike the little accumulation of misfortunes that the camera filtered and corrected. All conversation, all action became impossible, except of course police work, prison work, law, and photography, because nothing could be said or done that did not risk brushing up against a corpse, or referring accidentally to the deceased.

The photographer hardly noticed these changes; she was busy with her work. She lived by herself in a small apartment where, for the first time, there was neither the potential of visitors nor the memory of relatives to keep her company, high enough above the city that she could hear neither her neighbors' conversations nor the hush when one of them fell ill. Understandably, the neighbors found her a little frightening, and kept their distance; those who knew of her avoided her completely, afraid that she would catch them in one of her pictures. And this went on until she was befriended by a young man who took an interest in her work and followed her to the sites of murders, suspected murders, suicides and accidents.

They fell in love at once, as each had no one but the other to talk to, and each had a great deal to say. In time the photographer revealed the secret of the despair camera, which she had never told before, preferring to pass her pictures off as the work of talent. The young man, who had rather more contact with the rest of the city, urged her to break the camera. He led her through the streets at night, to the squares where aunts had once sat with their nieces, licking ice-cream cones; he showed her the field where old men had played games with a ring and a stake, the theater where all the city had gathered to watch tragedies in the fall, soliloquies in winter, farces in the spring, and in the summer traveling cir-

cuses; he took her walking past the graveyard fence and the shuttered windows of the embalmers' shops, the hospital parking lots
and half-built towers and the munitions factory, all of them
empty.

Have I done this? the photographer asked. The young man said
nothing. Then I'll throw the camera away at once, she said, and
hurried to the nearest embankment. She stood for a long time on
the quay, holding the camera at arm's length, and found that she
could not drop it into the water. The young man offered to smash
it for her, but her arms refused to pass it to him.

Do you know what? she said. I believe I'll have to take it back
with me. Back where? the young man asked. Home, she said, and
explained something of the house where she had been raised. I'll
leave it there, she said, in a place where no one will use it again.
But it's impossible for me to break something that belongs to the
family. She hurried off, and did not come back.

For a long time afterwards, the young man wondered what had
happened to her, whether she had stayed in the house to guard the
despair camera, or discovered that she could not leave the camera
any more than she could break it, or could not find the house and
so wandered on in search of it, with the camera, forever. In any
case, the city was not changed by her disappearance. The dead
had clammed up long before; they accused no one and revealed
only the most trivial slights to the police. Office buildings went
up in the suburbs, and the old men passed their afternoons at the
dog track; the New Opera House filled to its highest balconies
with whispers and the shells of salted nuts; secret, deadlier munitions were prepared in caves in the foothills nearby. For nothing

in a city with so many inhabitants lasts very long, especially not silence. The citizens had soon learned to refer to the dead by new names, and to console one another in new ways for the losses they continued to feel.

—That's it, then? Frank asked.

—That's it.

Frank put his arm around the doll's shoulders. High above them, the moon had burned down; small and red, it cast an uneven light over the waves. The man in the fens must have found his way out, or drowned, or gone to sleep; in any case, his voice no longer reached them.

—Is it true? Frank asked.

—Of who? the doll replied.

—Of us.

—I don't know. It's hard for dolls to see what role they play in the lives of people. But I don't think we have much in common.

—Maybe not, Frank said. In any case, I'm glad of your company.

—And I of yours, said the doll. We don't give off much heat, and it's terrible always to be cold.

—That's what's important, isn't it? That we're glad to be together.

—That's what's important.

Frank leaned his head against the doll's hair, and pressed his cheek to her cheek, until one was cold and the other warm. Just before morning, the tide picked up the box, which Frank had left below the high-water mark, and carried it out to sea. Frank didn't notice until it was gone. He spent all the night enjoying the weight of the doll's hand on his thigh, the softness of her hair, and the clever articulation of her knee. His own joints cramped and chilled, but he was afraid to move, for nothing in the world could be more precious or fragile than the life which, on certain nights, animates the images of the missing.

—FRANK? A WOMAN'S VOICE CALLED FROM far behind the rocks. Oh, Frank?

—Frank! A man's voice joined in cheerfully, as though amused to be calling after someone. Frank! Hey! Do you really think he's here?

Frank tried to stand, but found that his legs, chilled, had stiffened in place. He pushed his back against the boulder and tried to stand that way, but fell, scraped his palms, and sat licking at the cuts until Evelyn and Conrad found him. They stared.

—Well, Conrad said, rubbing at his beard. Well well.

—Frank? Evelyn held out her hand. Oh! You're chilled. Don't move. She rubbed his face with her scarf, and blew on his hands.

—He's lost a little weight, hasn't he? Conrad remarked. Frank hadn't seen him since the afternoon when he'd painted the portrait of Conrad's missing brother, but it looked as though the interval had treated the watch-factory owner well—as

Frank supposed it must have, given that he was one of the revolutionaries who, if what he read in the papers was to be believed, had seized power, or at least its visible forms. Conrad's face had filled out, his white hair grown into a mane, and he wore the collar of his tweed coat turned up rakishly. He was still dressed like an industrialist, but like an industrialist who has not forgotten his bohemian days. —Who's your friend? Conrad asked, pointing to Monique.

—We work in the doll factory, Evelyn explained.

—Oh! Conrad said. Then Frank's come down in the world. Haven't you been painting?

—Ah, Frank said, brushing Evelyn's scarf free of his face, well, no.

—You should take it up again. A knack like yours doesn't come—

—Will you help me? Evelyn interrupted. Help me get him standing up.

Each of them took one of Frank's arms, and pulled him to his feet. They leaned him against the rock and kept their hands on his arms lest he topple to one side or the other.

—Frank? Evelyn said. I don't want to know anything. She touched his lips; her fingers felt very warm. Nothing. Just come back with me. You're cold. Frank. Don't think anything. Just come back, and we'll be warm.

—What's Conrad doing here? Frank asked.

—He was walking on the beach.

—We ought to call this the beach of the found, Conrad remarked.

—I was so . . . I asked him to help me look, and then it turned out he knew you. Frank? You never told me that you were a revolutionary.

—It was so long ago.

—Can't think where I've seen the doll before, Conrad muttered.

—Or that you had been to prison.

—I thought you might take it the wrong way.

—But, Frank! I—never mind. Don't say anything about it now. I've been looking for you all night.

Evelyn watched Frank with the same care which, he supposed, she must once have given the horizon on nights of fog: staring not into his face but past it, trying to push aside all distracting shapes to make out the ship which might or might not be about to wreck. —Conrad! Help me carry him to the car.

Conrad tugged at Frank's arm; when they had got him a half-dozen paces across the sand, Frank turned. —But the doll . . .

—We're going to quit the factory, all right? We won't think about the dolls anymore.

—We can't leave her.

—Conrad, no! But the engineer had already dropped Frank's arm and gone back to Alpine Monique, to brush her hair from her eyes and arrange her hands in her lap.

—Oh! Evelyn picked Frank up as she had been trained to rescue waterlogged mariners, by draping his arms across her chest and his legs across her back; but Frank struggled until Evelyn put him down again. —What? she said at last, looking at Frank with mixed concern and contempt. What is it?

—She looks just like the photographer, doesn't she? Conrad said. What was her name?

—Photographer? Evelyn asked.

—Prudence, said Frank.

—She took pictures of what? Buildings?

—Corpses.

—Corpses? Frank?

—You drew her, Conrad said. On your walls, the pictures? Ha! That's it. Then my memory's not completely shot.

—So you drew her, Evelyn said.

—I was in love.

—I see.

—But she disappeared.

—The doll looks just like her, though, doesn't it? Conrad said. Of course I never saw her in the flesh.

—It's not her, Frank said.

—Oh?

—No. It's just a doll. I mean, not just a doll but . . . a doll all the same.

—Pity, really, said Conrad.

—Oh, I don't know. She's not so bad.

—Frank? said Evelyn. Don't you want to go look at the houses?

—Houses? Frank thought of the photographer's house, its turrets and wine cellars. Only with an effort did he remember, brick or wood, the seaside plots they'd agreed to visit, the question of the spare room. —Yes, of course.

—We'll leave the doll here, all right? Someone will find it. It doesn't matter.

—No, said Frank, let's bring her along.

—But—

—We'll take her in my car, said Conrad.

—Oh no, we couldn't impose, Evelyn said.

—I insist, the industrialist said, beaming. Anything for an old comrade.

Carrying Alpine Monique between them, Frank and Conrad stumbled up the stairs to the top of the cliff. Evelyn followed, her shoulders thrown forward, fighting off an impalpable wind.

Conrad's car was parked in a clearing not far from the road. —It's just like the old days, he chuckled as he fumbled for the keys. —I used to drive everywhere at the drop of a hat, when we were in hiding. Where can I take you? But let's have breakfast first, shall we? We'll stop somewhere on the way.

Frank and Evelyn nodded noncommittally and climbed into the car, Frank in front and Evelyn in the back seat, with the doll. A picture of a wide-mouthed woman hung from the rearview mirror. —Your wife? Frank asked.

—Alas no. My wife volunteered, poor thing, in the textile museum. I told them not to shoot, but with all the noise in the street . . .

—I'm sorry.

—That's my latest. A stenographer. Something, isn't she? She's even better in real life.

They followed the thin coastal road to a spur of the highway and joined the morning traffic. Green signs pointed the way to the various provinces. Frank thought of the deforester and his flight south; he wondered what the man had thought when the reporters' cameras caught up with him in one city and the next. Had he smiled more each time, knowing that he was out of reach of anything but pictures? Or had he forced himself more and more to put on the semblance of happiness, to hide his despair even from himself, so that no camera might see what he did not wish to show? In the back seat, Evelyn maintained a silence to match the doll's. She stared out the window at the suburbs, rolling hills bristling with uniform boxes of pink and white concrete.

The buildings grew around them and the highway forked, became a boulevard; they passed through the neighborhood near the bus station, the first part of the city Frank had seen. He remembered how magnificent it had looked to him then, the electric signs, the cafés and fountains, what a life they had promised! He sank back in his seat and closed his eyes, remembering his first days in the city, the garret, the photographer of the dead.

—Hnff! Nnff pmff!

Frank opened his eyes. Conrad had stopped at an intersection, and the manager of the doll factory, who was crossing the street, was thumping on the roof of the car. He pointed at Frank, at Alpine Monique, at Frank again.

—Nnff gmff!

—Frank? Conrad said. Who's *that*?

—He's from the factory, Evelyn replied. It's because Frank stole the doll.

—You didn't!

—Yes, he did. Didn't you?

The manager rattled the door handle and kicked the wheels.

—Why, Frank, Conrad exclaimed, you're a regular hell-raiser. Only what should I do?

—Drive, said Frank.

—Well, *this* is something! The car screeched and lurched ahead, leaving the manager in the middle of the street, shaking his fist and bellowing inaudibly. —I haven't had such fun since . . . oh dear.

The manager had caught the attention of a passing police car; he gesticulated to the officers and pointed at the fleeing suspects.

—How much is that doll worth? Conrad asked, pointing to the sandy and somewhat bedraggled Alpine Monique.

—Um . . .

Behind them, a siren came to life. The traffic on the boulevard had grown sluggish; Conrad wove as best he could between trucks on their way to market, tourists and Sunday drivers, and a convoy of long trailers carrying bundles the size and shape of small houses, wrapped in flapping sheets of canvas. The police car gained on them at first; then it, too, got stuck, and hung a few cars back, its lights flashing and siren ululating. One of the policemen rolled down his window to yell at the obstructing vehicles. Frank caught sight of a leather hat in the mirror, blanched, and turned to get a better look. The hat belonged to Fallow; beside him, Mac-Dougall, red-faced, pounded on the horn. Frank thought for a moment about what would happen to him if the detectives caught up, as they surely would.

—Turn here, he said, pointing to a side street.

—What?

—Turn!

Conrad spun the wheel and the car veered, nearly obliterating a bicyclist, into a narrow street. They rattled on uneven pavement around a traffic circle, past a park where the trees had begun to flower. The detectives seemed for the moment to have lost their trail.

—What is it, Frank? Evelyn demanded.

—Weren't the police all replaced, after the revolution? Frank asked.

—Only the chief, Conrad said. Where were we going to find new policemen, after all? They need special training. But tell me, where are we going?

—Bellaway's.

—What?

—It *is* spring, said Frank. Isn't it?

The sign in the boardinghouse window read WELCOME JUDGES! Frank rang the bell and a porter he had never seen before—probably he'd been hired to handle the overflow of guests—answered. The porter gawked at the unlikely assemblage of people and doll which stood on the doorstep.

—Can I help you?

—I'm looking for the judges, said Frank. When the porter hesitated, he added, —I'm an old friend of Mrs. Bellaway's.

—Ah, said the porter, they're not here. Never during the day. They're at the Hall of Justice, convening. They'll be back for dinner. By God! he swore. What a mess we've had, this week. Do you want Mrs. Bellaway?

—No no. Just stopped in to say hello. Nothing that can't wait.

—Oh?

Frank shook the porter's hand to forestall any questions.

The Hall of Justice was in the part of town which housed the ministries and the big hotels. A long staircase in the imperial style led up to a deep portico, at the back of which were enormous doors of brass. The steps were crowded with what Frank initially took for petitioners until he saw their cameras and tripods: tourists, Frank guessed, posing for each other on the flanks of the stone sea lions which guarded the entrance. He stepped out of the car and motioned for Evelyn and Conrad to follow.

—I'd better not park here, Conrad said, and they agreed to meet him at the top of the stairs.

Just then, the police car swung into view.

—Hurry! Frank tugged Evelyn up the steps, and Conrad drove away, Alpine Monique sitting stiffly in the back seat. Still pursuing Conrad, the detectives' car nearly passed the Hall of Justice, then stopped. MacDougall and Fallow climbed out onto the sidewalk, where they stood, pointing openmouthed at Frank.

—Well! MacDougall cried. Well well!

—If it isn't the artist! Fallow said.

—It's not often that you get to arrest the same man twice, said MacDougall.

—Do they know you? asked Evelyn.

Frank pulled her inside.

Some time after its construction, the Hall was made over as a museum; a frieze above the entrance depicted the divine gifts of painting, writing, and song. Voices echoed off the vaulted ceiling, off the marble floors and pedestals and statues. The crowd inside was dressed in the bright costumes worn by sedentary people who travel. They stood in groups of fifteen or twenty, listening attentively to the guides who explained in their native languages the meaning of the various paintings and statues.

—On your left is the equestrian statue of Reginald the First, who lived eight centuries ago, and was famous for proclaiming laws from horseback.

Frank accosted the first bailiff to cross his path. —Which way to the judges' convention?

—In the Great Courtroom. The bailiff pointed toward the stairs.

—And here we have the stone plaque on which the city's first laws were carved. The laws, which were deciphered by a team of scholars from our Quadrilateral University, are not unlike the ones used by the scholars in their own work, which suggests that these tablets refer to other, older tablets that have unfortunately been lost . . .

By the time Frank reached the top of the first staircase, his legs ached and his chest burned; he leaned against the balustrade, breathing shallowly and avoiding Evelyn's accusatory stare.

—This is a portrait of Hugh, the great ecclesiastical judge, famous for the doctrine that, as no two crimes are alike, so there can be no uniform system of punishment, a guide said.

MacDougall and Fallow interrogated the bailiff, who pointed upward. Frank staggered on, hugging the wall; Evelyn followed. —How do they know you? What did they mean, arrest you twice? Frank? What did they mean? The detectives? Frank?

He brushed past old portraits, so dark that their subjects could hardly be made out: improbably small men, dwarfed in fact by their robes and elaborate black headgear.

Fallow looked up at Frank almost with sympathy and called out, —You can't get out that way! Hey! Come back down!

— You're only hurting your own case, you know, MacDougall shouted. Resisting arrest!

The portraits on the second staircase were even older than the ones before; they showed judges of antiquity with the faces of infants against a background of blue tempera and gilt.

— This is the portrait of Forenses, an ancient judge from whom we get our word *forensic* . . .

Fallow reached the second floor, his handcuffs jingling.

Frank crossed a carpet of red plush, passed walls wainscoted in dark wood, and stumbled into a warm room where the air smelled of piss and chewing gum. Evelyn followed.

The Great Courtroom was awash in black robes. They filled the gallery and the balcony and nearly overflowed the tables for the prosecution and defense. Three or four sat behind the judges' bench, squirming and pushing one another from side to side, so that now and then one of the judges would fall off, only to get up, yelling indignantly, and push his way back on. Frank understood the tiny figures in the portraits outside: the judges were children. The oldest of them was no more than nine or ten; the youngest were so small that they had to be held up to the railings of the gallery in order to watch the proceedings. A trial seemed to be in progress; a judge, acting as the lawyer for the defense, reminded the court in a faltering soprano of the laws regarding evidence. In the witness box was a doll whom Frank recognized from the factory floor: the Countess Malconfit, dressed in a floor-length gown and mourning locket; she held her parasol in one hand and in the other hand a leash to which a toy terrier had once been attached. At the defendant's bench another doll, one

of last year's Soupape the Inventors, fidgeted with pen and notebook; his red hair stuck out engagingly from the sides of his
head, and his pink hands were etched with real acid and stained
with simulated ink. In the pews behind the defendant, a hundred
other dolls looked about incuriously. Frank recognized a half-
dozen Harvest Queens, Nurse Echelles, and Swimming Gwen-
dolyns, fully waterproof and capable of blowing bubbles for up
to half an hour; Condolences and Intrepid Williams, hunting
dolls and pious dolls and burly dolls with real chest hair, which
were apparently popular overseas. They drummed their carefully articulated fingers, blinked their eyes and tapped their
spring-loaded feet in no particular time on the parquet. When
the lawyer was done with his evidentiary wrangling, the Countess was sworn in.

—Your name?

—Marie Malconfit.

—Enumerate your parts.

In a singsong voice which seemed to emanate directly from her
chest, and in fact did, the doll listed the limbs and wires, the
springs and interlocking pieces of plastic, rubber, and china,
whose assembly Frank knew intimately; then she anatomized her
character in the same manner, declaring with neither modesty nor
self-consciousness that she was honest to a fault, dutiful, short-
tempered, generally unaware of the presence of others, deter-
mined, frequently unhappy for no discernible reason, and easily
discouraged from travel.

—What was your contribution to the welfare of the house-
hold? the lawyer asked.

—My name, the Countess said, and my unwavering loyalty.

—Aha! someone said behind them. You see?

MacDougall and Fallow had arrived, flushed and out of breath; they lifted their hats and wiped the sweat from their foreheads. Fallow held a pair of handcuffs. —Do you want to put these on, or shall I?

—Did you make a financial contribution? asked the lawyer, with all the contempt of a child to whom cynicism is still a novelty.

—But . . . Frank backed farther into the courtroom; the detectives followed, as did Evelyn. —These are the judges?

—You can see, MacDougall said, why we don't much bother with trials.

—I contributed my entire life, said the Countess Malconfit.

—These are the real judges? These children?

—Well yes, they're as much judges as any other judge, if that's what you mean. Haven't you ever seen one before?

—They have the power to try cases? To separate the guilty from the innocent?

—Yes, if you want to put it that way, yes.

—Were you ever unfaithful? asked the lawyer.

Frank had retreated as far as he could; he bumped against the rail which separated the spectators from the proceedings. —Good, he said, and raised his voice. —Your honors!

A thousand tiny faces looked at him.

—Ssh! whispered MacDougall. Can't you see they're busy?

—Your honors, I have a case to bring before the court.

There was a great murmur of small and curious voices. The children on the bench discussed the interruption, evidently not sure how to proceed. Fallow stood where he was, still holding the handcuffs but not, for the moment, trying to attach them to Frank's wrists.

—A case? the chief judge said at last. What is it?

—Your honor, I accuse myself of making pictures of the missing.

—What? said MacDougall.

—And of stealing a doll! Fallow said.

—What? said Evelyn.

—Of the who? said the chief judge.

—Don't bother with him, your honor, said MacDougall. He's deranged.

—Explain yourself, the chief judge commanded.

Frank told his story as best he could: how he had received his first commission, his technique, the number of portraits he had made. He told them how he had been arrested and put in prison without a trial, how he had been thrown in the prison cellar and how he had escaped. I did take a doll, he said, but she was mine. He explained about Prudence and his drawings. The judges on the bench listened patiently; the lawyer-judges and spectator-judges were rapt, as though they had never before heard anything so interesting. —Do you find me guilty? Frank asked.

—I don't understand, said the chief judge. Who are the missing?

—Why, they're the ones we miss. The ones we look for.

—Yes, said the chief judge impatiently, but before they were missing. Were they dolls?

—No, your honor, they were alive.

Chaos seized the courtroom once again. Judges pointed, shook their heads, pushed each other and were pushed in return. Fallow scowled all the while, rattling the handcuffs.

—I still don't understand, the chief judge said. Are you alive, too?

—Yes, your honor.

—Then this court has no jurisdiction, the chief judge said.

—What?

—We cannot try the living.

—But . . .

—Your case is dismissed. You're free to go.

—But I'll be arrested!

—Well, said the chief judge, we can't do anything about that.

Frank thought about it for a moment. He looked at Fallow, at MacDougall, at Evelyn, who looked back at him curiously. —Well then, he said, I'm a doll.

The judges on the bench, the lawyer-judges and spectator-judges all looked at Frank, rapt, for a moment, then burst out in a hundred whispered conversations. The ones nearest Frank repeated what he had said to the ones behind, who repeated it to their neighbors, who must have heard it wrong, for the older ones giggled and the younger ones pestered them for an explanation; the babies among them wailed their incomprehension and soaked their robes in drool. It would mean a great deal of work, Frank realized with some satisfaction, for whoever had succeeded him in Bellaway's laundry. Torn-off corners of yellow paper circulated through the balcony, between the defense and prosecution, up and down the bench; each judge wrote something, and in the end all the notes were passed to the chief judge, who leafed through

them, then summoned the judge playing the lawyer for the prosecution, who explained something in a whisper. Paper airplanes covered in jargon and precedent drifted from the balcony to the bench.

Through all this, the Countess Malconfit maintained an aristocratic detachment, hardly aware that her testimony had been interrupted. Soupape the Inventor rubbed his ink-stained hands in mock distraction.

The chief judge by means of gavel blows and a good deal of shouting called the rest to order.

—We don't believe you, he said. Enumerate your parts.

—All right, said Frank. He paused. How many parts make up a life? He remembered a few terms from his prison anatomy: the philtrum, the temporal bone, the sciatic and the optic nerves. If only he could consult the old diagrams pinned to the walls of his cell, he might name them all; but there would still be his character to consider. What were its parts? He had become what he was, but he could give it no name, not now, not with fifty grubby faces grinning at him and pulling the corners of their mouths up with their thumbs. —I . . . Frank began, faltered, stopped, began again, was still.

—Well. The chief judge yawned. Hurry up.

—Yes, said the prosecutor, it's not like *you* were our only case.

—I . . . Frank stammered, —I . . .

—You have to give him time to prepare, said Evelyn. He's entitled to that, isn't he?

The lawyer for the prosecution was against this; he protested at the top of his lungs, but was shouted down by the gallery, who evidently found Frank amusing, and wouldn't mind seeing more of him. The chief judge was won over; he allowed that Frank's trial would continue as soon as he returned with his parts properly enumerated. He was warned, however, that the process of enumeration was complex in the extreme, and that the slightest procedural mistake would be grounds for the dismissal of his case. The lawyer for the defense recommended that he consult a textbook on the subject; there were many in the library of the Quadrilateral University. Because the procedure was so complex, he was granted an indefinite amount of time to complete the enumeration, and the gallery wished him good luck with it.

—Now then, Fallow said when it was over, and approached again with the handcuffs.

—Wait! the chief judge ordered. If he's to be tried, then he can't be imprisoned until the trial is done. You know that, detective, don't you?

Fallow admitted with great chagrin that he did.

—Then you're free to go, the chief judge told Frank, and named a figure for his bail. It was quite low—but then dolls weren't expected to carry much money. Evelyn paid it without looking at Frank.

Spitballs and laughter followed the detectives out of the courtroom. Frank and Evelyn descended the carpeted stairs, past the dioramas where schoolchildren gaped at tiny murderers defending themselves against tiny accusations, the famous trials of the past.

Conrad was waiting on the steps of the Hall of Justice, declining to photograph tourists. —What happened? he asked.

Frank and Evelyn shook their heads in unison.

—I don't want to know what that was all about, Evelyn said.

—You saved me, said Frank. Thank you. He tried to take her hand. Everything that had happened in the Hall of Justice seemed unreal to him now, as though he had wandered off in his sleep some time ago and only just returned. He could hardly remember what had happened since he left the factory the day before, except that it involved a bus. Frank understood two things then: first, that the world can be made to disappear only by purely senseless action; and second, that understanding always comes too late. Orestes was right, he thought. Evelyn pulled her hand away. Frank might have been seeing her for the first time, there, in the midday light. Her face wasn't bad, though there were more lines in it than there had been when he first drew her with her sisters, sitting in Bellaway's parlor. It was a strong face, which had borne many disappointments, and seemed capable of bearing many more.

—I'm sorry, he said.

—I think it's better if we don't see each other for a while.

—All right.

—And if we consider the engagement over.

—All right.

—I'm going north for a while. And, Frank? I think . . . There's a sanatorium in the hills, where all sorts of people go. You could rest there for a while. It has a natural hot spring. Run by nuns, I think. I'll come and visit you, Frank, if you go there. All right? I'll visit you and we can see.

Frank agreed. It was as though he were having a conversation with someone else, some sad new woman who was lost to him even before the beginning of their acquaintance.

—Then goodbye. Evelyn pushed her way through a crowd of bird photographers come to take pictures of the storks which roosted on the parapets of the Hall of Justice. In seconds she had disappeared.

—Well! *That* was an adventure. Conrad looked at his watch. But now it's getting toward five o'clock . . . The industrialist held Alpine Monique sheepishly in one arm and with his free hand tapped his pocket watch. —And I have to pick up Leila . . .

—Leila?

—The stenographer. Very punctual. But what a figure! So if I can drop you anywhere?

Frank rummaged through his pockets and was surprised to find that he still had the scrap of paper on which Rosalyn had written James's address.

—I STILL CAN'T BELIEVE THE JUDGES WERE children.

—That's right, I couldn't believe it myself. Little children.

—Do you think they're born that way? James asked.

—Little?

—No, judges.

—I don't know, said Frank.

—And they try only dolls?

—What else could children try?

—Lots of things, Isabel announced. Just wait.

James and Rosalyn lived at the top of a wooded hill where tents served as houses: ropes had been tied between the trees; dropcloths and tarpaulins were draped over the ropes to make a roof and walls. The floors of the houses were clumsy platforms of wood, and the streets little more than paths that had been cleared between the trees. A factory sprawled at the foot of the hill; the air was rich with smoke. It was midafternoon when Conrad dropped Frank off at the end of the city's pavement. He found James's tent by asking directions of the neighbors, who stared mistrustfully at him and at the bedraggled doll he carried in his arms. They pointed uphill in silence and retreated behind the flaps of their tents. James was playing guitar in a clearing when Frank arrived. He looked afraid at first, then surprised, then ran across the clearing to embrace Frank. —Rosalyn! he called into the tent, which hung between two trees like a collapsed bird. —He's come back!

Frank spent the afternoon explaining what had happened to him since prison. Then Isabel returned from foraging and demanded that everything be explained again in greater detail.

—You were right to run away with the doll, she said.

—But, Frank, it didn't really speak, said James. Did it?

—It spoke to me.

—Do you still love her? Isabel wanted to know.

—The doll?

—No, the woman.

—I miss her. She's gone.

—Do you love her more than you love Evelyn?

—Stop asking questions, Rosalyn said, and eat.

She had made a stew of onions and tough green shoots that tasted of coffee; they ate and drank wine until their heads ached from the factory smoke. Isabel showed Frank her collection of automobile parts and vacuum tubes; she laid the bits of metal on the grass and explained where each one would go in the submarine which was, as yet, only a design in her idle afternoons. In return, Frank offered her the Alpine Monique doll. Isabel touched it, delighted, and turned it this way and that to see how it might best be taken apart.

—Do you want to live here? she asked.

—Or at least stay for a while? You look worn out, James said.

—I'd just be in the way.

In the end James had to agree. —But you should come with me to the parade tomorrow.

—Parade?

—It's the anniversary of the new regime. I'll be in Cathedral Square, playing guitar, if you want to come listen. In any case, it'll be good money.

The day of the missing, as it became known later in the city's history, when the revolution had been forgotten but the masked paraders filled the streets in greater numbers than before, marked the first day of summer weather in the city. Already by morning the exhaust from the buses and cars of the arriving visitors had condensed into a rust-colored haze, which left a fine black powder on the roofs and windowsills. In the streets, the air smelled of brackish river water. The sun rose red and stayed red; in the evening, it settled, bloated and fatigued, over the ocean, and for a quarter of an hour turned everything blue and orange-gold.

Frank left James just after dawn in Cathedral Square, between a band of ragged flutists and a nervous knife-juggler, making his debut that day, who reminded Frank a little of his old cellmate Smith. He turned down James's invitation to stay among the performers. After admiring the Human Weather Vane, an old man who climbed to the top of a wooden pyramid and balanced there on his big toe, pirouetting slowly to winds that existed for him alone, Frank wandered toward the parade route. It ran from the mountains to the ocean, from the terraced slopes of the zoological gardens down through the linden trees of the university arboretum, through the city's historical districts, and finally to the ocean, where new piers had been erected on the ruins of the old. The entire life of the city was concentrated along this line: those who didn't march stood on the sidewalk or hung from lampposts, windows, trees, watching those who did.

The first thing Frank saw, coming out of an alley, was an enormous fish, or rather a car disguised as a fish, driving slowly down the middle of the street. Mermaids followed, and fishermen casting hookless lines into the crowd, then another car hidden within a wave of papier-mâché and blue bunting; then came buses decked out as ships, and vehicles made up to look like buildings, bridges, statues, fountains, arches, churches. Floats represented each of the revolution's various battles. Some were monuments known to everyone; others were sheds, towers, pump houses, the secret landmarks known only to those who have lived in a neighborhood for a long time. About half of the paraders wore masks which depicted human faces in all their expressions: delight, horror, surprise, annoyance, fatigue, despair. No two faces were alike. Old men wore the heads of children, and children the faces of pox-scarred beggars; grandmothers shuffled through the crowd with furrowed foreheads of pioneers, and fat boys swayed back and forth with the disdainful eyes of postal clerks. It was impossible to say what their real expressions were, under the masks. They staggered, but it might as easily have been drunkenness as fatigue; they waved their arms in the air, but it might have been an imprecation; those were either wails that Frank heard, or the bleating of horns. Frank thought again of the doll's story. Was it his fault that Prudence had disappeared? It hardly mattered. In

any case she was gone. Frank couldn't bring her back, not even as a drawing, not anymore. He was alone, the only thing left for him to do was to enumerate his parts. The procedure was complicated; he would need time and quiet. He would return to the country, he decided, to the boarded-up house he had left, if it survived, and if not, to another like it. He would buy himself a supply of notebooks from the stationer's by the bus station, where he'd bought his first sketchbook, and some of their deep blue ink, which surely he wouldn't be able to find in the provinces. With the money he'd made at the doll factory he could buy all that and have enough left over for a bus ticket. He would go soon. Tomorrow, perhaps, yes, Frank decided to go tomorrow. Today he wanted to enjoy the parade. The masks were exquisite, he thought; the citizens must have spent all year preparing them. He could almost recognize the nose on this one, and was sure he'd seen the face on that other before. And that wig! Frank laughed. He watched the masks pass for an hour or two; when he could no longer resist the desire to praise them out loud, he turned to his neighbor, a stout and kerchiefed woman who held the handles of a laundry cart full of ice. —Aren't they wonderful? he said.

—Who?

—The missing. I mean, the masks.

—What?

Frank blushed. —The masks. The faces of the people who disappeared under the old regime.

—Tourist, are you? She winked. Not familiar with the local customs?

—But . . .

—All mourners in the city wear masks. Because it's bad luck to take too lively an interest in the departed. They watch us, that's why, and if they see that we're more interested in them than we are in our own world, they spirit us away. Would you like a cold beer? She reached into her laundry basket.

—No thank you. Frank pushed his way out of the crowd, not wanting to see the float representing the prison, which, judging by the gunfire at the end of the street, was about to arrive.

Frank wandered. He followed the river past the houses of the old families, where high stone walls hid the lower branches of flowering trees; he crossed empty squares where the statues of once-famous composers presided over gardens of pebbles and pigeon dung, and other squares with wells in them, and shuttered windows. The shops were closed, and the sidewalks were empty; the citizens were all, he assumed, at the parade.

The boulevard rose and fell with the last of the stubborn hills that had resisted leveling and the quarries that had disgorged white stone for the Cathedral at the very beginning of the modern era or the very end of the era before, Frank wasn't sure which. This part of town seemed populated entirely by dogs. They barked at him from behind palings of green wood and painted fences; packs of mutts ran out of alleys to sniff his feet, nip at his ankles, bark, growl, and turn away, satisfied that he would not stop within the lines they had marked out with their piss. Farther on, the factories began, set far back from the street; their smokestacks poked at the sky like an acupuncturist's needles, trying to relieve some celestial malaise with machine parts, boots, keys, kites, nails, cars, rails. Freight cars sat on their sidings, ready to carry the city's varied products into the forests of the north and the cities of the east; to the villages along the coast and across the plain where Frank had been a child and through the mountains which marked his childhood's horizons. As far as the rails ran, so far ran the city, and beyond it lay only stories told by the train men. Frank turned back, his legs aching, toward the familiar parts of the city. He lost his way, and soon walked between tall metal constructions and boxes of poured concrete which bore the imprint of their wooden forms. He had come to the modern part of the city.

Frank could go no farther; he stepped through the first revolving door that responded to his touch. Almost at once he was sold a ticket and hurried through a turnstile to a long gallery of marble floors and white walls. Not paying much attention to his surroundings, Frank sat on a bench and closed his eyes. He opened them some time later, and found that he was looking at a picture of a child dressed in a blue-and-yellow shirt, who looked back over his shoulder with fearful curiosity. His chubby hands held the straps of a green knapsack embroidered with a grinning dog. Behind him an orange sky descended over canted roofs; a streetlight somewhere to the left of the picture cast a shadow that might have been a bicycle against the side of a house. Frank stepped closer to read the descriptive plaque next to the frame. *"Portrait of Saul.* Late in Hugo's life, the city itself is subjugated to the psychology of the individual. Having begun with the premise that people seek to escape from life, he arrives inevitably at the conclusion that we see what we want to see, although our wishes are often obscure to us. *Saul* and the other late works, through their subjectivity, achieve a kind of universality: the distant bicycle and the crooked alley implicate us in Saul's flight; they are disquieting

landmarks in the city of our desires." Frank looked at the picture
for some time and wondered how the curator could have mistaken something so simple. He studied two or three pictures
more, and found no trace in them of anything but what they were,
pictures of the missing. Someone must have seen that; someone
must have seen them, and understood. Then Frank remembered
the revolution. Perhaps the pictures had served their purpose
after all, he thought, whatever the curators said about them. Suddenly hungry, Frank walked out of the Isinglass Museum into the
festivities of the evening.

He had been drinking for a long time and riding the buses at
random, climbing down from one as soon as it intersected the
path of another. He saw the Cathedral two or three times, and
thought kindly of the nuns praying in their huddled collectivity
to their distant God. He went over and over the river; once he
reached the bus depot and had to find a bus that was leaving. Each
time Frank left a bus he bought a paper cup filled with beer,
brandy, wine, coffee, whatever the nearest stand happened to sell.
By the time he staggered off the last bus, which, the driver informed him, was the last of the evening, he no longer had any idea
where he was. On a road by a forest. By the water. Ahead of him,
a domed and luminous café overlooked the ocean. Blue-and-
yellow parasols flapped like pinioned butterflies on its can-
tilevered balcony; colored lights limned the spires of the dome,
the eaves, the arbor's lattice. Menus scrawled in soap on the plate-
glass windows cast illegible shadows on the thickets that ringed
the parking lot. The café looked as though it had been left there,
in the shadows of the pine forest, by mistake, a child's toy aban-

doned at the end of a birthday party whose theme had been so inventive that the children would be disappointed by all parties to come, until they understood that they had no choice but to grow up. The sign above the door, repeated in gold tracery on the windows, read: FINN'S. A golden dolphin arched its back over the name. Frank suspected that he should go to sleep; he would have to get an early start the next day if he wanted to get everything ready for his departure. Then there were goodbyes to say, to James and maybe to Mrs. Bellaway as well, for she'd been kind to him, at times, in her own way. But he was drawn to the lights; he walked the little way that remained between him and the front door. Inside, a few revelers were prolonging the holiday into the early hours of the morning: students in the marine-blue scarves of the Quadrilateral University, artists in coats of spotted fur, and maids in black frocks, night porters with callused hands just ending their shifts. A single waiter carried bottles to and fro. In the far corner of the room, the barman tapped without method at the keys of a player piano.

—To understand this story, you have to know that I was once a sailor and once a lawyer, said someone on the balcony. Frank threaded his way between the tables to the sliding doors at the far end of the room. Outside, despite the cold, water-scented wind, he found a circle of silhouettes with a bottle and an ashtray at their center. The one who had spoken was a short, white-haired man, leaning against the railing. In the moonlight, his face shone like the inside of a shell.

—I have seen many things that those who spend their lives in one place do not see, and I have heard many things that those who are not admitted to the bar do not hear. I have heard the confessions of the great murderers, and I have fallen in love with beautiful poisoners and corrupt counselors. I have condemned mad beggars to be burned, and bookmakers to be flayed alive, and all this in a land far away, where the laws are different from yours, and cruel punishments of every sort are admissible. I could tell you how petty thieves have the nails pulled from their fingers, or how dancers who strike displeasing poses find themselves sealed to the neck in molds of lead and left to atrophy in the public squares, or I could tell you how cocks and clairvoyants whose timing is off are boiled together at sunrise. But all these stories would be nothing compared to the punishment inflicted on the man who dared to fall in love with an automaton that happened to belong to the Emperor.

Frank sat quietly in one of the canvas chairs and waved to the waiter to bring him a drink; he closed his eyes and listened to the old man's voice, smooth like a lawyer's and rough like a sailor's, a voice in which any story might seem true.

The Inconstant Machine

You would know, if you had ever crossed the ocean, that the Emperor of this land collected automata of all sorts, but most of all those which had a human or mostly human form; he particularly loved those which imitated human imperfections. For instance, he had a steam-powered singer who sang only sharp notes, a mechanical smith that struck itself again and again with its hammer;

a spring-wound knight of brass that dropped its sword and tripped on its scabbard, and a hundred other clumsy machines that he would set going all at once, and watch until they had mutilated themselves and one another to the point where none of them could carry on. So I will end one day, the Emperor told his ministers, whom he assembled weekly to watch the automata destroy one another. If I am mortal, he argued, then the world is imperfect, and if the world is imperfect, then these machines are a perfect image of it. The ministers did not know whether to agree with the Emperor and admit that he would die, or to disagree with him and insult his automata. Invariably they hesitated, and were invariably put to death, for, the Emperor reasoned, what good is a minister who can't think on his feet? For this reason, the post of minister soon became undesirable. The days when it had been the privilege of the aristocracy to advise the Emperor ended, and the priests were recruited to fill the vacancies. At last the Church was forced to declare itself absolutely uninterested in all matters of state (which pleased the Emperor a great deal), and the merchants were made ministers, then the artisans. In the Emperor's old age, only uneducated peasants could be found to advise him on his foreign trade, his wars, his roads, the growth of his library and the taxation of his people. A woodsman named Frank was among those chosen by lot to go to the capital. Because of his familiarity with fire and axes, he was made the Minister of War, a quiet post, because the empire was then at peace, and in any case the Emperor took all military matters into his own hands. Frank was left for a week in the capital without much of anything to do. The days of ceremonial dinners and long lines of supplicants were long since over, as there was nothing to be got from a minister who would hold his post only for a week. The Minister's office in the War Ministry, formerly an imposing suite of rooms on the top floor, had been transferred to a small room near the lobby, where the current Minister might leave his overcoat and a few small bags, if he wished. Frank spent his week wandering the streets of the capital. He saw the markets, which I can hardly describe to you except by saying that nothing you can imagine was for sale there, yet all the stands were overburdened with goods. He swam in the river and lay naked on the bank, drank himself senseless and woke up on an island which, though he didn't know it, was reserved for the pleasures of the Emperor. It was there that he saw the automaton. She walked the island paths, singing to herself, just like an ordinary woman, though more beautiful and more regular of gait. Her name was Prudence; her flaw, for which the Emperor had chosen her, was inconstancy. She fell in love with Frank, if it can be called love, at once. She veered toward him and seized him in her arms, pelting him with kisses, which Frank, drunk as he was, found it impossible to resist. Soon he had learned her name and why she had been brought to the island; she did not, however, reveal her imperfection to him, but told him that she had been made unable to perceive the passing of time correctly. Frank decided to save her, and led her to the water.

Ships landed on the island every day to deliver automata culled from the various parts of the empire: the mining towns to the north where dancing gnomes were wrought in copper and feldspar; the river towns to the west where little girls were fabricated ingeniously from green branches, reeds, and tar; the port cities where the automata were given the semblance of cunning, and cut the purses of tourists. Ships came from the archipelago where all statues are sacred, and from the isthmus where, having no glass, they use automata instead of mirrors: if they want to wear a certain jacket, they try it first on their replica; they comb the hair of their double if they want to see what they will look like with a part in the middle or on the side, and this has the advantage that they can see experimentally, changing their image before they change themselves. Ships even came infrequently from the city, mythical now, where automata are built by other automata, who in turn build all the tools that the human inhabitants will need. In this city the machines have castes. At the top are those that have the least contact with humans: the machine-repairing machines, and the mechanical draftsmen who prepare plans for a machine so abstract that it will have no purpose at all, except to demonstrate the ideal toward which all devices aspire, that is, incomprehensibility.

Frank led Prudence to the port where the various ships were moored, and their cargo unloaded. In the confusion of the quay he found one of the captains, and identified himself as a servant of the Emperor, holding up the badge he received when he arrived in the capital.

Take this one back, he said, pointing to Prudence. The Emperor doesn't want her.

Doesn't want her? the captain asked. Why not?

She's perfect.

Nonsense, the captain said. Let's see her walk around a little.

Prudence stepped gracefully up and down the gangway, swinging her arms; she spun on one toe before the captain, bowed, and stopped.

Perhaps you're right, the captain said.

You can leave her at the War Ministry, Frank advised. For analysis.

The captain watched Prudence for an hour more, as his ship was unloaded; then, as he could find no fault in her actions, her words, or her bearing, he agreed to carry her back to the city, and Frank took her to the War Minister's office, where the two of them stayed happily for three days.

The night of the automata arrived, and Frank was summoned back to the island. A great number of machines had been assembled in a pit before the Emperor's pavilion: dancing gnomes with mismatched legs; cast-iron smiths with nervous tics; armatures of wire and springs that cringed in corners, miming agoraphobia; superstitious automata that crossed themselves ceaselessly and skipped over cracks in the pavement; and delirious augury machines that pointed to the clouds and cried, Enormous birds! Impending storms! in well-tempered voices of reed, brass, and wind. The ministers shifted nervously from foot to foot, not knowing what was expected of them. Meanwhile, the Emperor checked his night's players, to be sure each was wound up tight, at a boil, charged to capacity, ready to destroy the rest. The Emperor, I should tell you now, had already remarked on Prudence, and thought her the most wonderful of the lot. Her imperfection was at once the most subtle and the most rare: inconstancy had seemed the one defect that a machine could not simulate, for while the errors of humans are endless in their variation, the errors of automata are dismally ordered, and give at best the illusion of unpredictability. When the Emperor saw the inconstant machine for the first time, he wondered whether he should spare it from the weekly massacre. He even considered appointing the automaton to be his heiress, and in this way guaranteeing the empire an imperfect ruler for perpetuity. If he did not do this, it was only because he was old and set in his ways, and because he could not deprive himself of the pleasure of a magnificent automatonomachy, which, he reasoned, might well be his last. All this is to say that he noticed Prudence's disappearance at once. Every worker on the island was summoned, tortured, and interrogated; then the captains who had deposited cargoes there in the past week were dragged from their ships and taverns; in this way Prudence's fate was soon known. The Emperor turned to Frank. Where is she? he asked.

Frank thought quickly and then answered: She is no more. Because of her defect, she walked into the street and was crushed by a bus.

The Emperor sighed. An inconstant machine must want death, he reasoned, incorrectly, and as machines are the mirror of the world, it must mean that the world, too, wants to die. He foresaw the end of his empire, and his own end, saw his body rot unmourned, and his island become a peninsula with the accumulation of silt in the harbor, and his peninsula be overrun by souvenir hunters, and the souvenir shops sacked by barbarians, and the barbarians burned by priests, until no trace would remain of this pit, these stands, and this vast array of imperfect machines. He could do nothing to prevent this, nor blame anyone for it, but all the same he decided to punish Frank. After the automatonomachy was completed and the other ministers put to death, he retired to his room for three weeks and devised a punishment so ingenious that, if it worked, it would keep Frank alive forever.

·   ·   ·

—What was it? Frank couldn't help but exclaim.

—Eh? Who's that? Step forward. The old man lit a match and held it before Frank's face. —Who are you?

—Drunk, Frank said. I mean, Frank.

—Then you're in the right place.

—What? Who are you?

—My name is Felix. This is Gustav, and Alexander, and Bertolo, Paola and Françoise and Adolphus who we call the Dolphin on account of his having no arms. We're drunks.

—We're *the* drunks, Gustav emended.

—The last drunks, Paola said.

—The only drunks, said Felix. The only drunks anywhere.

—There must be others in the city, tonight, Frank said.

—The city! The city doesn't exist.

—What?

—Sometimes I wonder whether even this . . . Felix waved his hand at the ocean. But no, it's too dull, it must be at least a little real. You don't want to believe too much in anything else. Not in the road or the woods or the bus that occasionally comes but more frequently remains hidden. In fact, we live on an arid plain that extends as far in any direction as we care to look. But our minds can't bear the monotony. That's why we have to make up stories about the bus, the woods, the road, and the cliff. You follow? If I were to jump off this cliff, right now, what do you think would happen? I'd fall on my ass and get up for another drink.

—But the city . . .

—What would you invent if you lived on a featureless plain, but a city? An endless variation of landscape, a proliferation of

new perspectives, interiors, elevations. A place where you can re-
visit nothing, because you reinvent it all each night.

—That's not exactly true, Frank said.

—But you admit that the underlying condition of life is monotony.

—Well, then why stay here? If everything is unreal.

—Because they're open all night and I'm friends with the barman.

—And the story?

—Oh, so I don't sleep it off.

—But what was Frank's punishment?

—I have no idea. I just talk, and talk, and see what happens.
The trick is to go on for as long as possible.

—You must have been thinking of something when you began.

—I must have been thinking of something . . . Maybe. It's gone.
The Dolphin yawned.

—Listen, Felix said. You try.

—What?

—Tell us something. Edward! Get this, this Frank another
drink! Get us all another drink!

—But I don't know what to say.

—It doesn't matter what you say, it doesn't matter. Just talk.

Edward arrived with a tray and a fresh bottle; drinks were
poured. Felix shook the Dolphin awake, and he butted his neighbor and so on, until the drunks were all more or less alert; fresh
cigarettes burned between their fingers. Below them, the ocean
scurried through hollows in the rock, and fingers of foam shot up
toward the terrace. The sky brightened and the horizon became
distinct; weighty clouds advanced toward the city and the barman

fell asleep at last at the piano. Edward wiped the glasses and scrawled tomorrow's menu on the windows; there would be soup and dumplings and fish stew at a reasonable price. Frank stood with his back to the water. He wondered at the golden light inside the café and the sapphire light without; he turned to admire the ocean, and opened his mouth to begin whatever story would come out. The moon sank into the water and the tide climbed the cliff. Frank spoke, and spoke, and hoped that the next day could be for a while longer, perhaps indefinitely, postponed.

IT BEGAN WHEN, FOR THE SECOND TIME, I left the house where I had been a child. Not that, seen from the outside, it seemed any great loss: nothing about the weathered walls, the shingles sliding by degrees from the peaked roof, the tilt of the front steps, or the gently sagging boards of the porch held the eye. It was an old house; there were others like it; when the last of them had fallen down, new ones would doubtless be built. Nor did the inside of the house, seen through an upstairs window, hold much to grow fond of: a tilted table and cracked chair, walls of peeling flower-patterned paper stained brown with rust and trickling water. A water closet. A sink. A stove and fireplace. A map of the night sky. And what was there to be seen from inside the house, if there were anyone to see it? Two men nailing a window shut. Two men in dusty black suits and shirts recently whitened, now smudged with the dirt from their hands. The taller of the two, hammering, peered again into the room, his forehead

THE ARTIST OF THE MISSING

furrowed with concentration lines. His scholar's face, his faint brown hair and long neck, went badly with the body huddled in the suit—all joints, it seems from this perspective, and all of them bent, as though for some time he had been trying to climb into a small box, and had only now given up the attempt. And the other? He held the tool case, humming. Beyond them, a plain of cracked mud tufted with weeds extended as far as anyone could see in all directions, except to the south, where low, distant mountains separated this country from the next.

When I finished hammering, we climbed down from the roof to inspect our work. We'd drawn the deadbolt and barred the cellar door; we'd boarded over the downstairs windows and nailed the upstairs windows shut. The house seemed a blind and unwanted thing now, waiting at the end of its road to be flattened by the wind. It might have been a century since anyone had lived there; it might have been a house from the sad, sinister stories James's father told on the nights when lightning reached up from the plains to revenge itself on the parching sky. This is what I thought as I followed James up the road to the place where, sometime that afternoon, the bus would pass on its way to the city.

1995–98

ACKNOWLEDGMENTS

To Abie Hadjitarkhani, Cyd Harrell, Dan Horch, Maureen Howard, Tracy Stampfli, and Herb Wilson, the first readers; to Jori Finkel, without whom this book would never have seen the light of day; to Jim Reinhold, Paul Toney, and the habitués of the Casa Paraffin, for their friendship; to the Camargo Foundation, for giving me space; to Kevin Kopelson, for his perspicacious listening; to Jennifer Hengen and Charlotte Sheedy, for their faith and remarkable persistence; to John Glusman and Rebecca Kurson at FSG, for seeing what was missing, and to Amy Benfer, for making the ocean move.

Paul LaFarge was born in New York City in 1970. He studied comparative literature at Yale and Stanford, and has lived and studied in Paris. In 1998, he was a writer-in-residence at the Camargo Foundation in Cassis, France. His work has appeared in *San Francisco Magazine* and *Conjunctions*. He lives in San Francisco, where he directs the Paraffin Arts Project, an obscure vehicle for instruments of light.

Stephen Alcorn was born in the United States and spent his formative years in Florence, Italy. He attended the Istituto Statale d'Arte, an experience that left an indelible impression and infused his work with a passion for bold technical experimentation in a wide range of mediums. Mr. Alcorn's work hangs in numerous private and permanent collections, both in the United States and in Europe. His work has been the subject of numerous feature articles in *Print, Graphis, U&LC, Linea Grafica, Grafica & Disegno, Prometeo*, and *Abitare*.

Since 1986 Mr. Alcorn has lived and worked in Cambridge, New York, with his wife, botanical artist Sabina Fascione Alcorn, and their two daughters. The year 1993 marked the opening to the general public of The Alcorn Studio & Gallery, a multifaceted workshop featuring rotating exhibits of both artists' painting, printmaking, and publishing activities.

Those interested in acquiring the original relief-block prints adorning this book may do so by contacting The Alcorn Studio & Gallery, 112 West Main Street, Cambridge, NY 12816; telephone: 518 677 5798; fax: 518 677 2526; E-mail: alcorn.art@worldnet.att.net;http://www.alcorngallery.com

Dimensions: 19 × 13-inch image; 23 × 17½-inch paper
Hand-printed by the artist on acid-free paper

Per la Sabina, musa onnipresente.
—*S.A.*